LAWS of the GAME
L. M. Causey

© 2023, ISBN : 978-1-946766-75-5

Cover design by Jennifer Labelle

Illustrations by Winnchester

Published by
Romance Divine LLC

DEDICATION

To those who never thought this was a bad idea:

A.T.   D.R.   S.D.

&

KRH3 for being my rock and my balloon

&

Of course, my parents.

*"You never know how unhappy you are,
until you're not."*

L.M. Causey

KING CONSULTING HEADQUARTERS

PROLOGUE

My name is Alexandria Anastasia King. I'm an equal partner in a business people tend *not* to talk about, but everybody wishes they had on speed dial. I came by my money the old-fashioned way, at least in today's world. I was a starter wife. I helped my now ex-husband build the dream business he always talked about. The dream eventually became a billion-dollar monster. It came as no surprise, especially to me, when he named himself Founder, Owner and CEO.

A few years later he decided the next logical step was to leave me; supposedly to *find himself*. So, at the ripe old age of twenty-nine, I collected a severance package in the eight figures range and moved on with my life. He did eventually *find himself*. Unfortunately, or fortunately, it was at the bottom of a bottle without a clue on how to get out.

When I first met my ex-husband, he was a mess. He had no focus, but I could see the potential for potential. He came from blue collar divorced parents with enough sibling dysfunction to make any daytime talk show host drool. None of them ever aspired to be anything more than what they were. Now, there's nothing wrong with having no ambition, but it should never be a family legacy. I gave him direction and kept moving him forward. Sometimes I felt like Sisyphus, but I kept pushing the boulder up the hill. After all, I was under the delusion I was working to make both our lives better. At the end

1

of our rainbow was a massive corporation with unlimited years of growth in its future. Eventually the beast was able to buy and sell its competitors at will.

The acquisitions were turned inside out and sold for ten to one hundred times more than the initial investment. When my ex decided to pull the trigger on our marriage, his reason was he still had so many other things to accomplish and felt my assistance was no longer necessary. Apparently, he was under the impression I was his fucking assistant.

To say I lacked sympathy during the divorce negotiations would be an understatement. We sat across from each other in one of the cavernous boardrooms, which I designed. Hell, I even picked out the hand carved banquet size conference table used to complete the final paperwork. I still believe to this day he felt his time was too valuable to pay attention to such a trivial proceeding. His attorney was completely outclassed by the men and women I had on my side of the table. Since he couldn't be bothered to pay attention, every time he checked his infernal phone, I asked for something outrageous. He waived his hand and told his attorney to give me whatever I wanted. He finally managed to put the damn thing down at one point and used his outraged grown-up-voice to tell the room he would give me whatever I asked for if I would stop trying to run his life.

The entire divorce would have been sad if it hadn't been so easy. The best thing I can say about him is he never cheated. I'm sure it's only because it would have taken effort and desire, which he lacked. Besides, I think somewhere in the empty boulder he called a head, he knew I would end him if I thought infidelity was even a possibility. This fear was probably his only redeeming quality.

When the divorce was finalized he went on a shopping spree. He bought all the things he claimed I would never let him have. When he was done buying the fancy cars and the one-of-a-kind motorcycles, it didn't take long for him to realize he had no idea how to run his own life. He lacked a single clue on how much 'grown up paperwork' is required, daily, to maintain the kind of wealth he was now responsible for. Thinking he knew everything, he never bothered to hire anyone to take over what I did for him and the company. Without proper guidance or direction, he didn't change anything I put in place, in his business or his personal life. When he mysteriously died a year later, I got it all. *Every. Damn. Cent.*

His estate retained fifty-one percent voting rights in the company and as the sole beneficiary, I ended up with everything. Over the next several months, I liquidated most of what I helped to build and then I sold what was left to his sniveling board of directors. Those narcissistic pricks had no idea I was the one who wrote the contracts they'd originally signed. I sold every one of his new toys and his million-dollar penthouse was on the market before the autopsy was completed. Ironically, he left me because he wanted to control his own life; but in the end I still made all the decisions.

I met Jack Sterling when my divorce was reaching its peak. He was my attorney's private investigator. I spent more time talking to him than I did my attorneys. We discussed everything from politics, to movies, to miscellaneous personal things. His job was to dig into the ex's life and find anything worth using during the divorce proceedings. When all was said and done, Jack found very little I didn't already know about. If I'm honest I'm the only one who knew where all the bodies were buried; in truth I buried some of them. I think Jack respected me even more when he figured this out.

Jack is former Secret Squirrel and you wouldn't know it by looking at him, but he's ridiculously wealthy. I think one of his relatives invented air or something. Given his family's fortune, Jack can work for peanuts doing exactly wants he wants when he wants. He can best be described as cantankerous. He stands at six-foot two and is more fit at thirty-five than most men are at twenty-five. People often mistake the salt and pepper hair for weakness. This would be their first of many mistakes. He looks like the offspring of Sam Elliott when he was in '*Road House*' and Max Martini, in any military movie ever. We became fast friends and found our views on the world were very similar. We also knew the wealth we had at our disposal could be used to do things most would never dream, much less dare, to take on.

Jack showing up after the ex-husband died is still something I remember like it was yesterday. The day after the cleaning service found the body, Jack was knocking on my hotel suite door. A part of me wanted to ask him if he had a hand in what happened, but in the end, I didn't really care. He came to see me with two pieces of good news. The first of course is obvious. The second was he finally had answers for me on what happened to Katie.

Jack was really the only person I talked to about her. I always felt he understood how upset it made me to know no one was ever punished for her horrible death. Katie was a very sweet, naive, young girl when I hired her as my personal assistant. She started as an un-paid intern when the business was getting off the ground. Her work ethic didn't change from the day she was hired. Her continued success with the company was done with hard work and loyalty. Before she died, she was earning upwards of six figures.

One weekend on her way to California, to visit a friend, her new car broke down. The car was discovered the following day by the Nevada Highway Patrol. It took another fifteen days before her body was found near the state line. I've read the autopsy report more times than I care to count. The ghastly things done to her are what horror movies are based on. Since she was found in the middle of one of the most desolate areas of the open desert, the highway patrol and local police really had a hard time making any progress. She didn't have any immediate family to speak of and since there was so little to go on, the case grew cold quickly. I paid for her funeral and for several private investigators to see if they could uncover who had done this to her. My ex-husband couldn't be bothered to attend the service, but he was more than willing to tell me he thought I was throwing good money after bad looking for a ghost. He often told me I needed to learn to accept bad things happen to good people. *What a dick.*

Jack was nice enough to tell me the details of the ex's demise. Of course, there is not much to tell when your cause of death is a cardiac event brought on by excessive alcohol. When he was done with the good news his face got serious and he sat me down. He proceeded to tell me he'd taken it upon himself to investigate Katie's case. He told me he had always been curious as to why the case had gone cold. Since she was special to me, this gave him the final piece of motivation he needed. Jack told me he'd cashed in a few favors with his friends in some of the various alphabet agencies. It wasn't long before he found out the case didn't stall but had in fact been road blocked. Jack was quick to point out nothing illegal was done. It was more about the people involved letting the case sit until it was no longer front-page news. Now, whether they were paid to do this is still unknown.

While there were still some holes in the story Jack told me, the result was the same. The ex-husband was skimming money from the corporate accounts and Katie found out. Instead of coming to me, she confronted him. Neither Katie nor my ex had any idea I already knew about the skimming. Sadly, Katie didn't ask me, and I never shared the information with her. I know she meant well and I'm sure she felt safe confronting him. After all, she'd been with me almost from day one and experienced all the craziness of our marriage from a front row seat. I suppose therefore I blame myself for her death. There isn't a day goes by I don't believe if I had told her I knew about his juvenile attempts to steal from the company, she would still be alive. Of course, when Jack tells me what else he found, I realized her death was ultimately my fault.

It turns out my ex-husband made some poor decisions and got in very deep with a local criminal entrepreneur. The skimming started so he could pay for whatever craziness they were up to. When Katie confronted him, he decided he could kill two birds with one stone. He decided to pay off his new business partner by giving him Katie as payment. Some of what Jack tells me is conjecture, but he believes it explains some of the evidence. Jack felt this is the only scenario that made sense.

My ex didn't do the dirty work of course. Based on some additional items Jack managed to find out about the car led him to believe the head of the ex's security detail probably damaged her car in some way. Then grabbed her in the desert and turned her over to the business associate.

Jack also tells me he's already done some sneak and peak on the man he believes killed her. The fruits of his labors were gruesome; he found out the man takes trophies. Jack pulls a small black velvet box from his pocket and hands it to me. Jack said he found five or six others in the guy's crash pad. When I open the box, I find a single earing. Katie wore the very same earrings every day. He said he remembered seeing her wearing them in a photo on my desk. I know without a doubt he found the monster who killed Katie. Jack doesn't disappoint. He tells me the villain in this story is none other than Raymond "Big Boy" Covington.

Almost as an afterthought Jack tells me of the demise of the ex's head of security. He apparently died in a tragic auto accident when his Escalade blew a tire in the desert. Jack said he died of dehydration. Apparently when the SUV flipped over it threw him out the window and subsequently landed on him. He was trapped alive under the vehicle. Since the road he was on is not heavily traveled, it was almost two weeks before anyone found the wreck. I have a strong feeling Jack facilitated the flipping of the SUV, but I decide to go with *don't ask don't tell*. When I was done processing all this information, both good and bad, Jack and I spent a few hours catching up.

We continued to meet every night over the next month to discuss the *unique company* both of us had been contemplating since we met eighteen months ago. Katie's unsolved death was a catalyst for a lot of our conversations in the beginning. Of course, Jack added some stories of other horrible wrongs he felt needed to be made right. So, we worked out every minute detail. Even with our unlimited finances there needed to be lines drawn in the sand, so to speak. In the past year Jack had been reaching out to men he'd served with and met in his travels. He had enough high-end candidates to start putting some basic services out there. Over the next few months we purchased the appropriate office and living spaces.

Some called us a security firm; some said we were mercenaries for hire or a personal protection service. A few people used fancy words such as Risk Assessment and Management. Jack and I liked to think of ourselves more simply as *problem solvers*. There was an *issue* and we would resolve it. Our methods would be to get the job done, whatever it takes. While we would cut corners and do what we had to, we would try to hold the moral high ground; although that didn't usually include those bad people we often encountered. The scum of the earth would feel our full wrath. Call it Karma; call it justice.

With the groundwork for the company in place, Jack started putting me through painful but necessary training so I could carry my share of the workload. I know, for a fact, some of the guys Jack brought in were clearly doubtful a woman standing five-six and weighing one hundred and fifty pounds could be anything other than a brunette sex toy. I also know they only gave me the benefit of the doubt because of Jack. However, it didn't take long for them to figure out what he already knew; I more than had the stomach for this kind of work. I earned their respect and loyalty one at a time. I took my share of punishment, but I made my point every time. Jack said I was a natural. However, given our line of work I'm not sure it was a compliment. With blood, a surplus of cash and the tragic death of a young woman, *KING Consulting* was born.

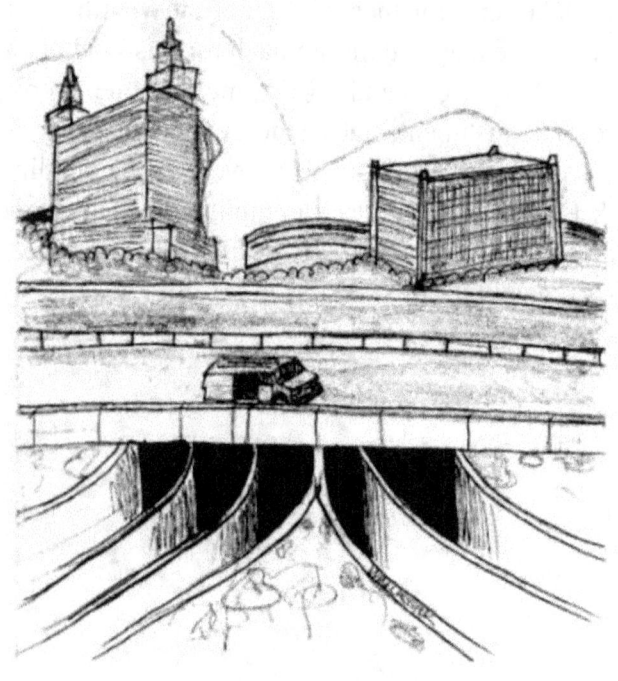

The Tunnels

ONE

Every now and again you find yourself in a situation where all you can think is, *'How the hell did I get here?'* Tonight, I find myself in exactly that position. I'm deep inside one of the giant drain tunnels around Las Vegas. Yes, it truly sucks, but we were in the middle of asking a local low-end pimp some very important questions when we came under fire. I must admit his favorite collection spot was not the best place for an interrogation. Also, to be fair, the guys shooting at us were looking for him too. We just happened to get to him first, lucky for us; finder keepers so to speak. Today started like any other day. I woke up, shot some people; they were paper silhouettes, but still. I did some work in my office and then I had a nice quiet lunch. Right before dinner I took a call and ended up being chased by these morons through the streets. The result is now we're taking cover under the city. It's not like I *want* to get shot at. I'm trying to get the answers I need from our guest. It doesn't help the situation much when we had to drag him into the tunnels with us.

Parts of our team took up secondary positions around our location when the shooting started. I don't know how many men, if any, we've lost in all this mess. I can accept wounded, but not dead. I know we need to get some answers from this clown and quickly. I tap my throat mic, "Are we ready to ask some questions?" The answer comes back in my earpiece immediately, "Yep." I give the signal, to the man at my shoulder, to keep a lookout. He nods, and I make my way past him. The three other men with him move up in position. I find Jack standing near a cutout about twenty feet down the drain tunnel.

"It doesn't smell good down here." Jack says as he shakes his head. Based on my look, he knows he's already told me this several times.

I can see the slight grin on his face. "What's so funny?"

"Oh nothing, I'm trying to see if I can collect on the bet."

Before I can inquire to the specifics he continues.

"The wager is, of course, how you're going to get this piece of horse shit to tell us what we need to know."

"How much are you looking at?"

"I think it was up to five large when we had to take cover in this romantic location."

"Jack?"

"Yeah?"

"You suck"

"Only when I must darlin', only when I must," he says on a smirk.

I punch him in the chest and walk into the cutout where three of Jack's team stand watch over our guest.

'Goldie' Monroe is a skinny fake Armani suit wearing low rent pimp. The only thing good about a bottom feeder like him is he picks up all the shit. So, if we squeeze him correctly we should get what we need. I often find people talk to people like him because they see them as disposable. He's currently sitting on the trash strewn ick-covered ground of the drainage tunnel. It's probably an improvement over some of the places he's been. His hands are bound behind him. His legs are spread and secured with rope to some nearby rebar loops poking out of the surrounding walls.

I look at Mikey, "Were you able to find anything useful in the truck?"

He shrugs. "I found some ice picks, will those work?"

"Mikey you're my hero." Poor guy barely fits in the tunnels. He's almost as wide as he is tall, and he stands about six-seven. When he opens his dinner-plate size hands I see four ice picks. I don't know *why* we have four ice picks in the truck. I mean it's not like we're making fancy drinks or anything. I take them and squat down in front of Goldie. "Tell me where your boss is, or I'm going to kill you and leave your dumb ass down here."

I see the slight twitch of his lips. I lean quickly to the side and he just barely misses me. However, the shot does land on Jack's boot. Exactly what he gets for standing behind me.

"The little fucker spit on my boot," Jack mutters.

I look up at him and before I can blink Jack rams the butt of his assault weapon into Goldie's fake gold capped grin. Hearing one tooth break is bad enough but hearing so many all at once makes you almost feel bad for the dumb ass.

Mikey quickly puts his hand over Goldie's mouth as I straighten up.

"Ok Goldie, let's try this again. Where's your boss? By the way, I want you to know if you so much as drool on me, Mikey is going to rip out your tongue with his bare hands and bitch slap you with it. Nod your head if you understand."

Goldie nods and Jack pipes in, "And they say you can't teach an old pimp new tricks."

I shake my head; Jack's the only man I know who can be in a sewer and still make jokes.

"Goldie, *where* is your boss?" I wave at Mikey and he removes his hand. Goldie leaks blood and teeth bits out of his mouth and looks at me. He mumbles almost as if he's trying to check to see if he can still speak with so many broken teeth.

Goldie wags his head from side to side. "I can't."

Mikey, with almost unreal speed, smacks Goldie in the back of the head and I put my hand up to stop him from hitting him again.

"Goldie, I'm not going to ask you again. You either tell me or I am going to make your last minutes on this earth very painful."

He looks at me and murmurs in a voice lacking any fight, "You gonna' kill me anyhow."

I look him directly in the eyes. "Yes, yes I am."

I reach out, with my triple gloved hand, and find both of Goldie's testicles inside his fancy burgundy suite pants. I'm a little surprised because if I was in his position my nuts would have crawled up into my throat by now, you know; if I had nuts. I put my hand up and Gavin hands me a ball-peen hammer from his belt. Before Goldie can grasp what is going on. I use it to pound one of the ice picks through Goldie's left nut.

Goldie starts to make a bunch of very unpleasant sounds. Mikey wastes no time and puts his hand over his mouth. I think more because Mikey didn't want to hear him scream.

When Goldie stills a bit, I pound a second ice pick into his remaining nut. Goldie starts to scream again and even with Mikey's hand over his mouth, his screams are loud. The blood has started to flow, and he must be on the verge of passing out.

"Nathan, do you have a stun gun on you?" I ask the Viking, because he looks like one.

"Yeah boss," he hands me one out of his cargo pants pocket.

I take it and find the wires are already attached. *Have I mentioned how much I appreciate these guys?*

Goldie' screams have now turned to whimpers. I do, however, notice his eyes are starting to roll around in his head a bit. I know I don't have much time to get the information we need. Gavin is kind enough to throw what's left in his water bottle at the pimp to make sure he stays with us a little longer.

Goldie seems to focus for a moment and follows my hands as I reach out with one of the wires. Goldie starts to scream but his words are muffled by Mikey's hand, so I motion for Mikey to remove it.

Goldie does his best to take a deep breath and manages to say, "H-he's at the top floor of the old Frontier."

All the hotels pretty much run together to me, so I look up at Jack and he shakes his head. As I attach the first wire to one of the ice picks, Goldie starts to cry and scream again. I can't believe we had to drag him all the way down here for this mess.

"I'm tellin' real. He's at the top of the old cowboy place!" Goldie screams repeatedly.

Gavin clears his throat, "Boss, I think he means the old Binion place."

Goldie looks up at Gavin with what can best be described as hope. He starts to nod vigorously. "The green one, yeah, yeah," Goldie squeals.

I look at Jack and he shrugs. This is pretty much the equivalent of him saying, 'I think this guy might be a fucking genius'. "Goldie, I don't think Jack believes you," I tell him as I reach out to attach the other wire to the second ice pick.

As Gavin takes video with his phone Goldie begins to weep uncontrollably. He starts to spill anything he thinks might save his life. This information will no doubt come in handy down the road. We'll look at the video later and see if there is any actionable information.

Jack relays the information to one of our teams driving around the strip and down town. They've no doubt been going a bit stir crazy waiting for us to tell them where they need to go. After a short wait, Jack reaches up to his ear piece. From the expression on his face our men have confirmed the intel, the piece of shit we are hunting is indeed at the top of the abandoned Binion Hotel downtown.

"Goldie, I want you to know this isn't personal. We really do appreciate all of your assistance." The look on Goldie's face might be relief. Almost as if he thinks he's going to live through this.

I turn to Gavin. "Are there all kinds of cherries and berries up there?"

"Yeah boss."

I hang my head and sigh, a running gun battle with some of Raymond's soldiers and now Las Vegas police are arriving. "Okay, let's get the hell out of here."

Mikey takes his gun out and puts it to Goldie's head.

I give him a hard look, halting him from pulling the trigger. "I didn't grab this guy's peanuts to let you shoot him. I'm curious to see if this works." I press the button on the Taser and the electricity pumps through Goldie's body. He convulses and gags a bit. Gavin looks a little green and I can tell Mikey thinks a bullet would save time.

"Really?" is all Jack says. Goldie slumps forward his entire body going slack as I release the trigger. The pimp is now leaking blood from several places. Not to mention it's starting to smell like cooked meat.

"Mikey, check him."

Mikey leans down, "Honestly boss, it's hard to tell."

I roll my eyes. "You just want to shoot him."

"Pretty much."

"Fine, shoot him. Make sure it's one through each eye. This will ensure the right people get the blame for this mess."

"You got it." He quickly fires twice and it's all over.

Jack touches his throat mic, "Let's go fellas."

The other four are patiently waiting for us at the tunnel opening. Jack leans in, "How the hell are we going to get out of here without being shot? You know Raymond's people are still looking for this ass clown."

I ask Gavin how far away our ride is. "Race says two minutes to pick up."

I'm hoping Race pulls up and we jump in without too much drama. However, looking around it doesn't really appear to be an option. Jack looks at me and almost seems a bit confused.

"Jack, I wanted to know where Raymond was hiding. I didn't plan to go and hunt him down after this. We need to regroup. I don't have a problem admitting I under estimated how many soldiers the bastard has. Good news is, I don't think we lost anyone. We'll deal with whatever injuries there are back at the house and make a proper plan. Like always."

Jack looks at me and grins. "You're a bitch. You know, right?" He nudges me out of the way to take up the second position at the tunnel opening.

I grin at his back knowing this is about as close to praise as anyone ever gets. We hear an engine and a few seconds later a car horn. Jack uses his laser pointer more for direction than for light. He aims it towards the sound of the horn. We can see the vague shadow of one of the transport vans on the bridge, but we would have to run through a kill zone to get to it. Out of nowhere a ladder drops over the opening of the tunnel. Then a raspy southern accent asks, "Hey boss, you need a ride?"

I quickly move around Jack to get to the ladder. I look up and see Joseph standing there all muscles, tank top and tight jeans. He's spectacular to look at but more importantly he can also be counted on for a good rescue. "Get us the hell out of here you hot bastard."

His bright white teeth are even whiter against his

dark, well-trimmed, beard, "This ladder is being held up by my junk, so you better hurry up."

I can hear the guys in the tunnel behind me laugh. Jack puts his boot on the bottom rung to keep it steady. I grab hold of the ladder and start to climb. As I reach the top of the ladder gunfire breaks out in the direction of the transport van. Clearly the plan was one of distraction and rescue. The last man up the ladder brings it up behind him. We make quick work of the distance between us and the second waiting van.

Race was a wheel man for about a minute until he was arrested. We bailed him out and he has worked for us ever since. He and Gavin came from the same neighborhood. Gavin felt, with some direction, Race would be an asset and he was right. As we get into the van, Race starts to update Jack and I on the injuries of the guys who provided cover as we went to ground.

"Boss we have four down, but none are fatal. Chucky may have a limp, but I'm not sure he didn't have it before he got clipped."

"Thanks."

"No problem, are we going straight back?" He asks as he looks at me through the rear-view mirror.

Head down taking a deep breath, I answer. "Yep, we need showers, food and sleep."

TWO

As we make our way through the city in the middle of the damn night, it only takes about twenty minutes to reach our buildings. Even the streets of Las Vegas have a slow time. Race makes his way down the long drive and scans his bracelet against the pad. The main door rolls up and he pulls into the cavernous garage.

Jack slides open the van door and we mostly fall out from sheer adrenaline drain. We all head to the hardware cage. Visiting Mr. Oliver is always the first stop after a job. Jack and he go way, way back. Probably as far back as when Moses had fifteen commandments. He doesn't say much unless you don't turn in something. Then it could get ugly. In fact, it'd probably result in an intrusive cavity search. He's as strange as he is smart. We leave all our guns and other weaponry with him.

Donna is in the garage somewhere. I can smell her cooking, but I haven't seen her yet. She must have brought down food for the mechanics. She's a little plump shaped Latino woman. Her dark hair and accent only add to her appeal as one of the most amazing cooks ever. She's also Jacob's wife, and thus has free roam of the buildings. As well as being the main cook for the masses, she also takes care of all our other wearable gear. Vest's and blood stains are her specialty. Given how many people we have on staff, she has many little helpers.

We don't have a lot of women who work for us. It

has nothing to do with having all the men to myself, despite what some may think. It does, however, have everything to do with finding the right kind of person to do the job. This kind of work is not for everyone, no matter the gender. There are things that we encounter that you simply can't *un-see*. And they stay with you.

Still, Jack and I are big believers in hiring the best person for the job, no matter the plumbing. But given what we do, there are many other factors that have to be accounted for before we can hire someone. That being said; we do employ a cadre of female contractors, mostly contacts of Jack and Eric's, veterans of many alphabet agencies, foreign and domestic, who we call on because of their specific and unique skill sets.

I stand in front of one of Donna's helpers and he starts to peel off my vest when I see a new face unloading our recently exited van. I don't remember hiring him, so my guard is immediately up. Shit! I really don't have the energy for another confrontation.

Jack senses something has caught my attention. He looks around and follows my line of sight and quickly makes his way over to me. He motions for the guy helping me to leave and he takes over.

"Calm down, I hired him last week. Remember Kenny and I had stopped by the bar we like. A fight broke out over shared oxygen or some random shit. I told you I saw a guy I thought we should look at. He whooped on three pretty good size guys all alone."

"Jack?"

"Yes?"

"What was *I* doing when you told me this little tale of yours?"

"You were watching TV and eating ice cream."

"Well, there you go. I was main lining mint chip. There's no way I was listening to you."

Jack tries to keep a straight face but can't manage it for more than a few seconds. "Fair enough, the surveillance video from the bar is in his file. You need to look at it."

I lean forward and put my head on his chest. "So, based on his bar fighting skills you felt putting him to work in the garage was the best idea?"

Jack finally gets my vest and compression shirt off. "Okay. Donna needed help and she can be very hard on the staff. I thought I would see if he could survive her first. So far, he's still alive. Not to mention Donna hasn't said she wanted to shave him and leave him on the curb. So, I think it's a win."

"Okay smartass, what's his name? He keeps looking at me as if I'm supposed to know him. So perhaps a formal introduction is in order."

"His name is Cane, with a C."

"Is it his first or last name?"

Jack laughs. "It's his *only* name. You know like Cher or Satan."

"Was he arrested for the fight?"

"Nope, when the cherries and berries showed up, Kenny paid the bar owner for the damage and we hustled out the back."

"Is he a good fit so far?" I ask, noticing Cane still paying attention to us. But I also notice he hasn't stopped working.

"Yeah, I think he's content for now. But we'll need to keep teaching him things if we want him to stay. He strikes me as the kind to take a bullet for what he believes in."

"Crap, pull up the video on your phone. Let's see what we can see."

Jack logs into our secure server. He brings up the video and hands me the phone. The scene starts calm enough. People are playing pool. The bar seems to be almost full. Every bar stool has an ass on it and there are even people on the dance floor.

After about a minute, a shouting match begins at the pool table closest to the bar. One of the large men gets pushed into a man sitting on one of the bar stools. The guy at the bar looks over his shoulder. There's no confrontation and I can't see any words being exchanged. The large guy still has a pool que in his hand. He pushes the guy sitting at the bar with enough force so the stool he's sitting on tilts forward. The guy at the bar, who I can now tell is Cane, reaches into his pocket and pulls something out. He continues to hold whatever it is at his side as he slides off the stool. With no fear he stands facing the guy with the pool cue, despite the other guy having a couple of inches, and about fifty pounds on him.

The pool cue guy lunges at Cane, who twists his shoulders and brings what now looks to be a black jack down across the man's jaw. The first guy hits the floor like a bag of sand. As the he goes down, Cane catches the pool cue. He then proceeds to swing it like a baseball bat. The second guy who is all gangly legs and arms goes down after a massive cloud of blood explodes from his face. The third guy who has a horrible reverse mullet tries to surprise Cane from the rear. There is a glint and

I can tell the guy has a blade in his hand. Cane takes care of this guy with a low mule kick to the knee. As the man crumples, Cane grabs his wrist and proceeds to break it with one quick thrust. He takes the blade from the guys now limp hand. Cane quickly moves behind him. He has a handful of his mullet in one hand and the blade in the other. He appears to be going in for the kill.

This is when Jack and Kenny step in. Jack puts his hand up and says something. Whatever he says convinces Cane to hand him the blade. Jack says something else and Cane releases the man's hair. The poor fool falls flat on his face. They both make their way towards the back door. Kenny meanwhile has thrown down a large roll of cash, I presume towards the man behind the bar. Less than a minute later, the police enter through the front doors as the three of them disappear out the back.

I find at the end of the video I have a grin on my face. Cane *is* extremely talented. I look at Jack with a bit of hesitancy, but I make my way to Cane to get my own first impression.

Cane stands six-four and weighs in at about two-thirty. He's all solid mass, no jiggle. Dark sandy blonde hair, a little longer on top, but nothing fancy. He has blue gray eyes; scruffy facial hair forms a closely trimmed beard and mustache. He has a wickedly strong square jaw. Not to mention there is some significant damage above his left eye. It's not a current injury, but I bet it's one hell of a story. At least he looks like he belongs. Clearly the guy has been trained in his duties. He is moving about quickly, efficiently and he seems to know where everything goes. To his credit Donna isn't yelling, in *any language*. Because she's not, he should be given a damn medal. As I get closer to him he turns to face me.

"Cane, is it?"

"Yes, Ma'am."

"I expect you in my office at eight tomorrow morning," and I walk away. I stop because I know better. I know I'm mad at Jack, not him.

"Cane?"

"Yes, Ma'am?"

"You still got the black jack?"

He pats one of the pockets on his cargo pants. I nod and head for the elevator.

KING Consulting owns a configuration of four high rise buildings. Each has its own purpose and covers a spectrum of businesses and functions. In our buildings you must have special permission from Jack or myself to carry a weapon. Jack is always armed. Also, each team leader can carry in the building if they so choose. However, no one visiting is ever allowed to carry a weapon into our buildings. I don't care if you're guarding the President of Mars. No one has a weapon without permission inside the premises. This makes things easier to control. Now this is not to be confused with the idea no weapons are available. There are accessible weapons all over the facility.

The top two floors of the main building are where I live. I exit the elevator to find Jacob waiting in the foyer, as I knew he would be. Jacob worked for Jack's family from the time he was out of diapers. He was part of the package when Jack and I got into business together. Jacob, if I had to guess, is about fifty-five or so but you would never know it. He's five-ten and almost bald. He speaks several languages. I'm not sure even Jack knows how many. He appears doughy, but not weak. He's extremely resourceful and can pack two weeks of clothes into a carry on. So, even if he liked to skin deer in the nude during a full moon, the man stays. When Jack and I combined our efforts, Jacob gravitated to me. Ever since, he has been my conscience and confidant.

"Good evening, Miss."

"Hello, Jacob, how was your night, any good porn on?"

"Funny as ever, Miss." Jacob has his hand out for my personal phone and any miscellaneous things I might have in my pockets.

We start to walk forward, and the large doors buzz open after I wave at the overhead cameras.

"Anything I should know about?"

"I am not aware of anything," is his answer. This, to me, means I should probably check in with my desk guys because something has gone to shit, and they perhaps are trying to clean up before I find out.

"Jacob," I let out a sigh, "do I really need to get into it tonight or can it wait?"

"It can rest until morning." His answer at least makes me feel better.

On the other side of the foyer doors two large desks flank each side of the entrance to my flat. At these desks sit very large men who are charged with my safety while I'm in residence. Some might think these guys are past their prime or not fit for the field. Absolutely the opposite is true. These are some of our most trusted men. They guard me as I sleep, and I have no doubt about their loyalty or ability. I just get to the door and the man to the right, Keith signals me. I wave to Demetri, the large scary silent man, at the other desk. He nods and keeps watching the monitors. I walk over to Keith and lean on the counter surrounding his desk.

"Boss, Eric needs to see you before you turn in."

I put my forehead down on the counter. "Call him please, I'll wait." I speak into the cold surface.

Keith picks up the phone and within a few minutes I can hear boots in the stairwell next to the elevator. Eric appears, not out of breath, but I know he was moving at a quick pace to get up to my floor as fast as he did.

"Boss."

"Talk to me Eric, I'm sleepy and I smell like Jack's tea."

Eric laughs, "Boss, I need to brief you first thing in the morning, if you have time before you get started for the day."

"Of course, for you I'll always make time."

I turn to Jacob, "I've asked the new guy from the garage to be in my office at eight. Eric, does this need to be secret squirrel?"

"Yes," Eric says, "but I think it would be good for the new guy to sit in on it since the old man thinks he will be a good addition for the teams."

"Sounds like a plan. Jacob, please make sure everything is in place for the meeting."

"Of course, Miss."

"Good night fellas." All I can think about is a shower and my clean sheets.

"Good night," they say in unison.

I must use more effort than usual on the doors which seem especially heavy tonight. They are steel reinforced, but a long night makes the bastards even harder to get open. My space, as always, is spotless and smells of clean laundry. In my bedroom the TV is on my sleep channel. My towels, as well as my night clothes, are out in the bathroom. *I love Jacob.*

THREE

I don't recall what time I finally went to bed, but it seems like the alarm is going off a few seconds after I get to sleep. I rub my eyes and make my way to the shower, since I know I have at least one meeting this morning. From what I recall from last night, I may have a possible unknown mess on my hands as well.

Heading into the main room, I can see Jacob has already delivered breakfast. Eric is at the table and he's not alone. Jack is sitting, stirring his alien tea as it stinks up my living space. He also has six stacks of hundred-dollar bills sitting in front of him.

"Why do you have to drink that crap?" I ask with a disgusted grumble.

"Because it bothers you," Jack grins as he slurps the stinky liquid.

"What do you know about what happened while we were out last night?" I ask as I scoop up three of the stacks of hundreds off the table, my winnings from last night's sear wager.

Jack puts his tea down and folds his arms over his chest. "First, why do you get half? I won the bet. Not to mention the little pimp spit on *my* boot." He held up his foot. "I need a new pair. Second," he gets serious, "Eric has informed me, one of the men from Team Three has been fucking our head shrinker lady."

"First, *I* touched his skanky nuts, so without me you

31

would only have dirty boots. Second, you're lucky, I only took half. As to *your* second thing, are you fucking *shitting* me?"

Jack cracks a smile as he puts the remaining three stacks of hundreds in his shirt pocket. "No, I'm not shitting you. Not to state the obvious, because I know you'll agree, but we need to clean this up and damn quick."

I stuff a piece of bacon in my mouth. "You think!"

There's a loud knock and Eric gets up to answer the door before Jack or I can say anything. He opens it and turns to us. "Boss, your eight o'clock is here."

"What time is it?" I ask no one in particular.

Eric looks at his watch, "Seven-forty."

"Well at least he knows how to be on time." I look at Jack and he shrugs. This is his equivalent of '*I told you so*'.

"Eric, let him in please."

"Yes, boss." He opens the door wider and Cane makes his way into the room.

"Good morning, Cane, how's your day going so far?" I ask to see what kind of answer I get.

He nods. "I woke up, had a good meal. So far so good." It's an answer, good or bad is yet to be determined.

"Cane, you'll shadow me for the morning." I see his face turn towards the door. "Don't worry. Jacob has already spoken to Donna and assigned someone else to work with her."

He seems to relax but only slightly.

"Jack, let's take care of this mess now before we start sorting through last night's op."

Jack pushes away from the table. "Works for me." He and Eric walk toward the front door.

I walk in the other direction and Cane seems a bit apprehensive until I give him a nod to follow me into the back elevator. He follows with caution, but without further question.

"Do you know what happened here last night while we were out?" I ask him

"No, Ma'am." He continues to look straight forward.

I continue to stare at him until he looks at me. He seems a bit taken aback to find me watching him.

"Are you telling me the truth?"

He stands a bit straighter, "Yes."

I lean against the elevator as I feel it slow. I exit the elevator and Cane follows. The boardroom doors are open, but no one has arrived yet. *This pisses me off in a special way. If I am already there, when everyone else gets to the meeting, unless they are bleeding a lot, they're late.* As I take my seat Cane takes a position behind my chair slightly to my left. Since I'm right handed he's already ahead of the game.

Jacob comes in, looks around and shakes his head. "Drew!" he yells at the ceiling. Drew appears in the doorway within seconds.

"Yes, Sir?"

"Please locate the doctor and Mr. Kranston and get them here immediately."

A look of disgust comes over Drew's face as he notices why Jacob is angry. "I will return with them, Sir." He disappears down the corridor. If Jacob is *my* brain, then Drew is *his*. He is a large, but oddly delicate man. At six-six, bald and easily three hundred pounds, Drew strikes an imposing figure. People underestimate him at their own peril. He could rip out your insides and then use them to tie you up like a Christmas goose. However, I think he finds assisting Jacob more suitable to his disposition.

Jack and Eric make their way into the boardroom. They look around the room and Eric lets out a low whistle.

"Do you think they're together working on their stories?" It's a rhetorical question and I address it to the room.

Jack looks at me, thinks about the question for a second and smirks, "I doubt it. If they were smart, we wouldn't be having this fucking meeting to begin with."

I nod at his answer and turn in my chair to look at Cane. "This is your chance to go back downstairs. No one will question your decision." I pause, "After this your options become very limited."

Cane looks at me and nods his head in understanding. He doesn't move so I assume he knows things are about to get real.

I turn back in my chair and Jack of course has his stupid '*I told you so*' look on his face, again. Sometimes it makes me sad I don't have the option to beat him as one of my daily options. Drew appears in the doorway with Kranston by the scruff of his shirt and Dr. Morgan very close behind them. Drew drops Kranston into the nearest chair and Dr. Morgan hastily takes the seat next to him.

"Ma'am, Sir's," is all Drew says as he and Jacob exit the room. Eric closes the large double doors behind

L. M. Causey

them. He un-holsters his weapon as he takes up a position in front of the doors.

Not surprising to anyone in the room Dr. Morgan is the first one to speak. "What is the meaning of this, your man was so rude when he burst into my office, *unannounced.*" She has the nerve to put an emphasis on the last word as if her time is far more important than anyone else's. I look at Jack and roll my eyes.

"Hello, I asked a question?" Dr. Morgan says trying to make eye contact with everyone in the room.

I slam both hands onto the thick wood table, "Sheila, perhaps you should shut your cock sucking pie hole until you know why you've been brought here." The good doctor has the nerve to look appalled.

The door behind me opens as the twins make their way into the room. I see in my peripheral vision Cane has come alert. I turn, look at him and wink. He relaxes, but only a bit. The twins are two very large men who really have no use except for the one I hired them for. Sometimes you must only be good at one thing to make a living in this world, find your niche and work it. In the case of the twins they have a rather ambiguous moral compass, one of their own design, but they are quite loyal. Cruz and Sebe have the ability of snapping a person's neck, cutting the body into tiny bits and disposing of the entire mess. No questions, no feelings and best of all, no regrets.

Kranston has seen the twins before and he knows something bad is about to happen to someone. I move from my place at the head of the table, so I can stand between Kranston and Dr. Morgan.

I keep my voice calm and professional. "Kran, are you having sex with Dr. Morgan?"

The doctor speaks up. "What happens in my treatment sessions is confidential and will not be discussed with anyone. I trust you know and understand even the most basic concepts of doctor-patient confidentiality."

I pull my knife from my pocket, flip it open and stab it into the table a few inches from where her pretentious French manicured fingers are tapping away nervously. Dr. Morgan makes a sound like a squeak and clamps her mouth shut so hard I can hear her teeth clack together.

"Kran, answer the question, if you would please," I say to the room.

I notice, as I made my way around, Cane is no longer in his original spot but instead he is slowly tracking me around the room.

Kranston puts his face in his hands and then looks up at Jack. "Yes, I have been having sex with Dr. Morgan."

Jack looks at him and shakes his head. "Boy, I don't care if you fuck a tree, a catfish or the doctor. However, I would strongly recommend you direct your answer to your boss."

Kranston looks around for me and finds me now in the corner. "Ma'am, I've been having sex with Dr. Morgan and I apologize for breaking the rules."

Dr. Morgan again finds her voice. "Alex, you *cannot* dictate how I treat my patients. *I* am the medical professional here, not you."

Jack laughs out loud because he knows I'm about to choke this woman with her overpriced Hermes scarf.

I push out of the corner and walk around to stand next to Jack's chair opposite the stupid woman. "Dr. Morgan, I'm going to take the little speech you just made as an admission of your guilt. Kranston, you know you can no longer stay here. You have two choices and you know what they are. You have one hour to make your peace and notify Jack of your decision."

Kranston looks down and takes a deep breath. He sits up and stiffens his spine. He quietly stands up from the chair, his legs shaking a bit, but he keeps it together. Cruz and Sebe quietly step to his side and nudge him towards the door.

Dr. Morgan seems to realize exactly what's happening as she is also aware of Kranston's choices. Of course, the joy comes for me when she realizes her fate isn't much better. She knows their only options are a needle or a bullet. Unfortunately, no one noticed her hand slide inside that large and overpriced designer bag.

She's out of her chair just as I thought she would be. She is lunging at me teeth bared and painted nails. But now her right hand is holding something small and black. A gunshot echoes in the room.

In one quick motion Cane is behind her. He brings her forward motion to a full stop by snatching her back by her hair. The knife I left in the table is in his hand. In one swift motion he slits her throat from ear to ear. Cane releases her hair letting her limp leaking frame fall to the stone floor. Her head catches the edge of the table with a thud and a small gun falls to the floor. Cane calmly folds the knife and carefully places it on the table.

During this exchange Eric has drawn his weapon and put it to Kranston's head. Even if he wanted to try to save her he has no choice but to remain still and watch his lover die. Out of the corner of my eye, I can see Jack has his weapon drawn as well. I had complete faith Jack would put her down no matter what her reaction was to the news of her fate. Hell, it was the plan we discussed earlier. We knew she'd react violently when she realized the penalty for her actions. Cane moved up the food chain by leaps and bounds by taking such bold initiative. As I look around the room, I notice one of the twins has made his way to the array of buttons on the wall, pushing the ones to summon Jacob as well as the cleaning crew.

Our company is a family, of sorts. Some say that blood is the best loyalty and that's one of our foundations…loyalty. We have each other's back and would go through a door with anyone in the firm. When people come on board it's a commitment. For life. Our retirement plan takes care of people to the grave. If they're loyal, that can go into extreme old age. If not…termination. Total termination.

Cane has retreated to a position against the wall. The entire scene doesn't seem to bother him. In fact, the pooling of the good doctor's blood at the edges of his boots seems of no consequence to him. Cruz walks Kranston out of the room without a word. Jacob comes in with the cleaning crew through one of the panel doors, as Jack holsters his weapon.

I turn to look at the shattered window behind me.

Jack bends down and picks up the gun. "Glock, G43, good for a lady's handbag." He removes the magazine. "Six in a single stack, hollow points." He looks at the window. "If she'd been more controlled, or a better shot, she'd blown that pretty head of yours clean off.

Maybe taken one of us before we'd put her down." He drops the gun and the magazine on the table.

"What the fuck!" I look at the gun and then at Jack. "She had a *gun*? In *my building*?"

Jack holds up his hands. "We'll check it out, find out what happened."

"What is this? Fucking *Oprah*? *You* get a gun and *you* get a gun and *you* get a gun."

"We'll handle it." Jack looks at me as if this is just another day at the office. "So, you ready to go over the cluster-fuck from last night now or do you want to do it later?"

I walk around the table avoiding the spreading blood pool. I pick up the knife and hold it out to Cane. "Take it, you earned it."

He puts the knife in his pocket without wiping it off.

"And Cane, thanks."

He merely nods.

I make my way over to Jack and he opens a panel door. On the other side is my private office space. Cane follows like a good shadow should.

In my office sits the team from the previous night's adventure. Even the injured men have been brought upstairs from the medical floor. In addition, the two teams who worked the street are present. They all notice Cane, but they know if he came into the room with us, then he clearly belongs. "Gentlemen, this is Cane," is all I say by way of introduction. They all nod and I assume he nods back. I don't turn around to find out. I take the seat behind my desk and Jack takes his place in his favorite crappy chair in front of my desk.

"Alright gentlemen let's hear it."

Casey steps up and begins to disseminate the information to the room. I make Casey do the briefings because he's so damn good looking. Don't get me wrong, he's a brilliant operator, but he's also wicked fun to look at, at least for me. Casey has a short business man haircut and very well trimmed beard. He has more muscles than I can count on both hands. Not to mention he wears shirts I'm sure he stole from a fifth grader. His sunset colored eyes are breathtaking, and the man has a thick, sexy, gravelly voice. He's our go-to when we need a Romeo for a job.

"Raymond 'Big Boy' Covington is, in fact, at the top of the old Binion's hotel downtown and he's hunkered down like some third world dictator. I'm fairly sure if he sees us make our way towards the building, he'll start throwing shit, and I mean literal shit, out the windows at us." The guys laugh because let's be real… They're guys. I make a 'continue' motion with my hand and the laughing dies down.

Casey resumes, "We would need to find a stealthy way to get into the building and there is a ninety percent chance he has the building wired. Getting up the stairs could be something like Indiana Jones, you know the first one with the damn boulder."

I shake my head and look at Jack. "Well old man, do you have any bright ideas?"

Jack looks at me like I'm speaking Korean. "Nope, got nothin'."

"A sniper would be the most ideal situation," Casey speaks first. "But the fool has covered all the windows with what looks to be wood and foil."

"Wait a damn minute," Jack pipes in sitting up a bit

straighter in his chair. "There's nothing in his profile to indicate he has any smarts."

Bronin nudges Jack in the arm. "He's paranoid of the mind-penetrating ray guns. The foil has nothing to do with smarts. The guy is as crazy as a bag o' cats." The whole room erupts into laughter.

Through the laughter I hear a voice say, "Ma'am?", but it's faint and I'm almost sure I'm imagining it. Then I hear it again and I realize it's coming from behind me.

I turn, and Cane seems to have something to say, I nod at him. "Speak up, Cane, don't wait for these clowns to shut their yaps."

"Yea, Ma'am," he clears his throat before speaking. "Why not bring the building down on top of him? If he already has it wired why not make it look like his own craziness caused the building to come down." The room goes completely silent.

Kyle slaps his knee and looks at Jack, "Someone give this guy a medal. He's fucking brilliant."

They all look at me and I look at Jack. Jack nods in agreement. There's something about a room full of guys eager to blow something up. All I can do is smile.

"Demolition it is." I dismiss all of them and hit the button on my desk for Jacob.

"Yes, Miss?" comes the voice through the inter-com.

"Jacob, please locate AJ and send him to my office. No rush, but I need to see him."

"Yes, Miss," and the line disconnects.

Kyle is holding the door and looks at Cane who is still standing behind me. "Cane, let's go." Cane doesn't move.

"Don't worry Kyle, he stays here for now."

Kyle nods "Okay, boss." He turns to exit and finds AJ standing, waiting to enter.

"Brother," he says as he holds the door. AJ pats him on the back as he enters the room and closes the door.

"You wanted to see me?"

"Yes, please make the necessary arrangements to set Cane up in one of the vacant flats."

"You want him on a particular floor?"

I think about it for a minute, "On second thought, put him in Jack's old flat with the connecting stair case."

"You got it, boss." He turns to Cane, "Let's get you moved in." AJ nods toward the door.

Cane moves past me placing his hand on my shoulder as he walks by. It's a strange gesture, but I think I get what he's trying to convey. AJ closes the door leaving Jack and I sitting there staring at each other.

Jack looks at the ceiling. "My old flat... Rather close for a guy who isn't on a team."

"I agree, but I think he has a skill set I would prefer to have very close rather than on a team floor."

Jack raises his eyebrow at me.

"You know damn well I'm not talking about *those* skills, you ass hat."

Jack laughs and tosses the folder he has been holding on his lap on to my desk. "Before we get to the folder, I want to talk about what we are going to do with Raymond. It's clear he's not the big evil he once was. Rumor has it he's high most of the time, seems to have become one of his own best customers."

I don't answer him right away. I'm too angry to speak and since yelling is not an option I take a deep breath and try to compose myself. "I wouldn't care if we found him in an ICU ward waiting to die. I'm going to end him for one reason and one reason only. Katie."

Jack winks at me and points at the folder. "The next one is a mess and a half. It has politicians, hookers and goats."

I throw a pencil at Jack as I open the folder. "Exactly how do we keep ending up on these jobs, I mean seriously, how many politicians can we help have accidental falls and/or gun cleaning accidents."

Jack chuckles. "You *do* realize if these people started to act human we would be out of work."

I resign myself to the fact he's right. As I read the file it appears we have yet another pervert who thinks he should not only be able to tell people of his respective country what to do, but now he wants to come to my city and attempt to do naughty things to children and perhaps goats. Damn perverts.

"I'm sure you have some ideas about how we should progress with this mess?"

Jack looks at me and decides to change the subject. "So, are you going to keep the kid as a pet?" he asks.

"What the goat?"

"Not the goat. Christ woman, Cane." He throws the pencil back at me to get me to look at him.

"Jack, let's put it all on the table. I'm not keeping him as a *pet*. I see the same thing you saw, and I think maybe I see it a bit clearer after the conversation with the good doctor. By the way don't let me forget we need a new one."

Jack sighs but manages to contribute, "We're definitely going to need a new damn table because Jacob is going to lose his shit when he finds the divot you put in it. If I remember correctly, the table was one of a kind. Maybe Jacob can get the artist to do something in stone or steel rather than wood."

"Not a *table*, a new doctor!"

Jack laughs, so I continue. "I think Cane will be a great asset and I believe his loyalty will only end with his last breath."

Jack gives me a look like he thinks perhaps I'm romanticizing the situation, but he doesn't disagree.

I ignore his look and continue reading the file about the politician and the goat.

FOUR

Jack and I spend the better part of two hours discussing the politician and what would be the best course of action. I was finishing up my notes for the file, when there's a knock on the door. Since neither of us asked to see anyone we're at a loss as to who it could be. The guys would not knock on a closed door unless something was wrong. I press the button under my desk to open the door.

Cane sticks his head in. "Boss, there's a problem in the lobby. Eric sent me to get both of you."

I close the goat file and nod at Jack. I take the time to grab an ASP out of my desk drawer and put it in my back pocket. Jack checks the load in his Glock and we start towards the elevator. Cane closes the door behind us and follows us down the hall.

"Cane, did you see what was going on?" I ask.

"Yea, a guy barged into the lobby as we were coming up from the garage and started making a scene. He spider webbed a few of the front windows."

As I press the down button on the panel, I look at Jack, "Tell our guys we're on our way and have them secure the area and call Metro PD. Please ask them to wait outside the building. We will be more than happy to escort the trespasser out to them." It's an unsaid agreement. We don't want the local cops in our lobby any more then they want to be there.

"On it," Jack hits the speed dial on his phone.

"Cane, please find Eric. Stay with him while Jack and I deal with this." Cane looks at me as if he's thinking about objecting. Then an understanding comes over his face and he nods. I'm not sure what he was thinking, but right now I'm only looking for his cooperation, not his opinion.

The elevator doors open on the ground floor. In the main lobby there is in fact what appears to be a large and, in all likelihood, smelly man. He's clearly pissed off about something. He has indeed managed to throw at least a couple of chairs at the giant picture windows. He's also screaming about something I can't make out from this distance. Out of the corner of my eye, I can see Cane has made his way over to Eric. The rest of our guys in the lobby are spread out. They have taken up positions between the elevators and the main reception desk. Jack and I make our way closer to the irate man and I can now begin to understand his yelling. Apparently, his wife left him and took his kids. I'm now beginning to comprehend what this is about. Domestic situations, always fucking dicey.

In one of the towers of our complex there are floors made up of several apartments. We use them as safe houses. In them we keep people who need a safe anonymous place to stay. In most cases it's short term while they get away from someone who is trying to hurt them. A good number of the people housed there are women and children who have been referred to us by local law enforcement. Since this part of our company is not publicized, and few know of its existence, my first question is how he even ended up on the property. There's a victim aide's office on the first floor of another tower and it could be this stupid fuck just got the wrong building. Jack stops walking as I continue to close in on our uninvited guest.

"Excuse me sir, is there something I can help you with?" He pauses his ranting and slowly turns to the sound of my voice. As he focuses his blood shot, beady eyes on me I see the rage in them.

"You stupid bitch, what did you do with my wife? I know you took her." He slurs all this and takes a wide sweeping punch at my head. He misses and manages only to spin himself around.

I hear a boot squeak behind me. I glance over my shoulder and see Eric has put his arm out to stop Cane in his tracks, like a mother holding out her arm in a car. I see Cane's jaw clinch. I wink at him and he halts his attempts to go forward. I turn back to the drunken guy who is still lumbering in a bit of a circle.

"Sir, your wife isn't here. I think it's time for you to leave. Perhaps the police can take you home."

He spins around again with a quickness I wasn't expecting, and I have to take a small leap back to get out of the range of his ham-size fist. I hold my arms straight out to the side to signal the men behind me to stay where they are. I can almost hear Cane's teeth grinding together. Clearly, I need to have a conversation with him when this is over.

Smelly guy starts to rant again, "I saw her come in here you whore. You're hiding her from me. With all these fuckers around, I'm sure she's banging most of them." He makes a lack luster sweeping motion with his giant arm at the men in the lobby.

I grin. I can't help myself. There's not a woman, or even a small group of women alive, who could take on the manpower currently standing in the lobby. I can, however, surmise we need more security when it comes to the people we have housed in our secure apartments. *Perhaps someone also needs to lose their job if they missed this drunken bastard following one of our charges back to the buildings. He's in the wrong place, but he may have only been a left turn away from being in the right place.*

"Okay, dumbass it's time for you to go. I'm tired and you're no longer entertaining." He lunges for me and I take the ASP from my back pocket and forcefully extend my right arm. The ASP locks into place. I swing it in a backhand motion and it contacts the moron's ribcage and a giant howl fills the lobby. He grabs his ribs, but he continues to come at me. I circle around and swing in a kind of forehand tennis swing and catch him in the knee. He goes down like the pile of shit he is. He rolls onto his side and puts his hands up as if to ask for a mercy. I shake my head in disgust. "I bet your wife begged for mercy at some point."

He looks at me almost confused. "I only did what I had to, to keep her in line," he says in a voice clearly reflecting the amount of pain he's in.

"Well, I'm simply going to do the same for you. Think of this as a learning experience. I mean you broke my windows and called me a whore. You're the one who clearly needs to be kept in line." I raise my arm over my head and I bring the ASP down with every ounce of strength I have right across his chest. The sound of the bones cracking echoes through the lobby.

He curls up in pain I'm sure in hopes of keeping me from hitting him in the chest again. This subsequently raises his head off the ground. I take this opportunity to bring the ASP down again. I catch him across the face with enough force to ensure his nose, both cheek bones and orbital sockets are surely broken. The blood from his face sprays my jeans and the shiny gray marble floor.

I lift my arm again and I hear Jack's voice. "Ok fellas. It looks like our friend is ready for some fresh air and I'm sure his ride is waiting for him."

I turn and see two Metro PD cars in the roundabout in front of the building waiting to transport our now profusely bleeding trespasser.

As if made of smoke, Cane is next to me and taking the ASP from my hand. He pounds it against a nearby pillar to close it and places it in one of the pockets in his cargo pants. He extends his arm in front of me as if to say, after you. I take his offer and head back upstairs. Stepping into the elevator, I realize I don't know who the guy's wife *is* or even if she's in our care. However, I do know a guy like him truly deserved a beating and he really needed it from a woman. I was happy to oblige.

Cane follows me into the elevator and inserts his new pass key. The secure access panel opens. He stabs the button for the top floors, my flat, smart man.

The elevator doors open at my floor. Cane steps out as if to check for additional drunk smelly guys. I step out behind him and the two men who occupy the desks outside my flat stand up and look a bit confused.

Cane walks ahead and reaches for the handle on the doors but finds none. He turns to his right, "Open the door, please."

The man currently with the power to open the door glances at me and I nod ever so slightly. He reaches down and pushes the security lock which pops open the door. Cane pushes the door and steps inside. He looks around and nods his head as if to tell me it's clear. I'm following his lead mostly to observe his behavior. I must admit it is proving very informative. He quietly shuts the doors behind us. As I move across the room I turn to find him standing in front of the now closed doors in what I can best describe as some version of a modified parade rest. I look at him and it's as if he was always supposed to be there.

"Cane do you still have my ASP?" I ask him as I flop down on my giant squishy over stuffed couch.

"Yes."

"Good, I would hate to think I left it on the floor with the smelly guy."

I reach for the blanket on the top of the couch and pull it over me and close my eyes. *There's nothing better after beating someone up then a nap.*

*****

I wake up and have no real idea of how long I'd been out. I do know however it's eerily quiet. There were no phones ringing; no knocks on the door and no intercom blaring at me. I turn over to check the door and Cane bless his heart is still standing there in his over watch position.

"Cane, do you have magical powers?" Upon hearing my voice, he seems to power up like a sleeping computer.

He looks at me and focuses, "No, Ma'am."

"Well, I think you must since I managed to sleep undisturbed for more than fifteen minutes. What other explanation could there be?" My blanket falls to the floor as I slowly stand up.

He looks at me and grins. "I texted Mr. Sterling and told him you had clearly decided to take a nap and he said he would have the tech guys shut down your rooms. My phone went dead shortly after I received his text."

"Thanks, I needed the rest. If you would please, call the old man, Jack." I explain in case he doesn't know who I mean. "He's probably spent my nap time at a strip joint."

Cane looks at me and it takes him a beat, but he realizes I'm probably kidding. He smiles, all be it only slightly.

As I walk into my bedroom I tell Cane. "I'm going to get cleaned up. Would you please locate the great and powerful Oz and ask him to lift the force field?"

"On it." Cane opens the door and I hear him tell the guys outside what I said. There's a bit of laughter which tells me he told them exactly what I told him. As I brush my teeth I realize the blackout must only be inside the walls of my flat because I hear the squawking of a radio on one of the outer desks. Then just like magic things within the flat start to come to life. Of course, this also means my phone is about to lose its mind.

I finish up in the bathroom, pick my phone up off the table near the dressing room and unlock it. I find a bunch of texts from Jack and some other miscellaneous pieces of information. I scan through them and leave the phone on the side table.

"Alex?" I hear Jack from the other room.

"What?" I yell back.

He must have come in from the back stairs. I would have liked to have seen Cane's reaction to Jack's entrance. When I don't get an answer from Jack, a small part of me wonders if Cane subdued him. I come out of the bedroom and Jack is sitting on one of the barstools and Cane seems mildly annoyed.

"I take it you came up the back stairs?" I kick Jack in the leg as I walk past him.

"Yep." Jack winks at me.

"Cane," I turn to him.

"Yes, Boss," he says through what I'm sure are gritted teeth.

"Why didn't you shoot Jack when he came through the door?" You could almost feel the tension leave him.

He clears his throat before answering. "Mostly because he's already really old and I figured pointing a gun at him might put him over the edge." Cane says, raising one of his eyebrows.

I laugh because he has balls and he's a fast learner. Jack snorts because he knows Cane *could* have killed him. I have no doubt Jack was set back on his heels when he found Cane standing guard inside the door. Cane, on the other hand, I'm sure let Jack live because killing the old bastard would have upset me.

FIVE

I grab a water out of the fridge. "Okay you two, we need to get Raymond's building down tonight. Let's put all our cards on the table so we can work through this."

I start to make my way to the back stairs. Without missing a beat Cane follows me. Jack is spinning on the barstool like a giant child. Cane alters his line and takes a very subtle step towards Jack. He deliberately bumps the stool causing Jack to rib check the bar.

Cane didn't say a word as he reached me at the door. I turn to look at Jack. I can't stop laughing and Jack has a look on his face of annoyed respect. I lift my hand up to Cane's head and lightly poke his temple. "Not just a target." I wink at him and he smiles. It's good to see, mostly because it tells me he's at least part human.

Jack collects himself and follows us down the stairs rubbing his ribs. I turn to say something as we enter the boardroom, when it dawns on me I haven't told anyone else we were meeting. However, I can see Jack has had his crazy elves hard at work, as everyone is already in place.

"Ok, what's the plan fellas?" I ask the room.

Eric places his fingers in his mouth and whistles to quiet the room. He's the leader of Team One and his height of six-six makes him a dominant force in any space. His voice is on the range of Ving Rhames, so when he speaks everyone listens. He has the remote for all the TV's in his hand. He pushes a few buttons as I take a chair at the table beside Jack. Cane remains behind me even though I have pushed a chair towards him. One of the giant screens comes to life with a schematic of our target downtown.

The clear and obvious problem is the building was built during a time when permits were more of a recommendation than a requirement. Not to mention the many questionable owners over the life of the building have made changes and modifications these plans will not show. No one would ever know all the nuances unless they were to go floor by floor and map it out. This tells me we're making plans on educated guesses and we will have to be able to make some decisions on the fly based on what we find. Eric is moving through photos and explaining what must happen. He covers in detail each floor as well as each entrance, exit and the roof.

I glance at Cane and can tell he has something to say. I knock on the table, "Eric, hold up a minute. Cane has something he would like to share." Eric looks over my shoulder and tosses the remote in Cane's direction.

Cane reaches out and catches the remote just before it reaches my shoulder. Eric for a split second looked concerned the remote might hit me. I give him credit for collecting himself before anyone else could notice the chink in his armor. I wink at him as a sign of faith. Cane moves around the table and clicks back through some of the photos. He begins to give his recommendations for the best places for our explosives team to put the charges. He wants to make sure we can get the most 'bang' for our buck. He also makes suggestions as to how many men we will need at each entry, on the roof and on the ground in support.

I can't really tell if this was something he did in another life or if it's something he comes by naturally. I make a mental note to find out more about where he came from after we finish with this building. Cane, in addition, asks several detailed questions. I can see the other guys instantly take note of his obvious knowledge. They give him respect as each of his questions is answered. Other team members make some suggestions and modifications they feel would enhance his initial comments. Cane seems to fit in like a missing puzzle piece we didn't know we were looking for.

The phone on the conference table starts to ring. I can see on the display it's our 'information desk'. I push the speaker button to answer the call and a voice resonates through the room. Kevin, our 'information desk', used a lot of drugs in his previous life and because of it most of his brain cells are mush. The good news is he retains the trust of people who are still in the life. In our line of work, it can be hard to get people to trust you. Sherlock has his street urchins; we have Kevin and his connections. Lucky for us Kevin is our way in and it doesn't hurt when people know giving him good information makes money appear. There's also the reassurance and proven promise there will never be any blow back on them, so it makes for a good relationship.

"Boss, I've got something you need to hear. You know the old guy tells me to call if I hear anything. He came and gave me a card with Raymond's information. I know what it means. You know the old guy?"

I cut him off because I know if I don't, I could end

up listening to him say old guy another ten times. "Kevin we're in the middle of something, can this wait?"

"Uhhhhh that's a negative, yep you need to hear this right quick."

"Crap, okay Kevin let's hear it." I don't speak harshly to him. He's sensitive.

"Ok, so Serendipity called me, you know her right, Boss?"

I lean my head back and close my eyes. "Yes, Kevin, I'm assuming you're talking about the hooker not the ice cream parlor." There's silence at the other end of the line.

My poor guys in the room want to laugh, but they know if they do it will not end well for them. "Kevin, the hooker called, what did she say? Was it about Raymond?" I finally say on a long-exasperated exhale.

There was another beat of silence before Kevin's manic tone starts again. "Yeah, Boss, she told me Raymond has a very large stash of cash in his building with him."

I lunge forward to hit the mute button and look around the room. "Anyone know anything about this?"

They all look at me and I know this is the first any of them were made aware of this. Of course, they also know this is going to put a huge fly in our ointment. I hit the mute button again. "Kevin, get the hooker to meet you and we'll pay her for her information. Same deal as always. Deacon and Max will go with you."

He starts to giggle, "I'm on it. I did good right?"

"Yeah, Kevin you did real good."

I pick up the phone, throw it against the wall and look around the table. Deacon and Max take it as their cue to go and pick up Kevin. The rest of the guys start to clean up some of the maps and papers on the table. Cane looks at me and raises his eye brows in question. I nod towards the chair next to me. He takes a seat and rests his elbows on the table staring at the TV's on the opposite wall.

I pinch the bridge of my nose as I collect myself, so we can begin the discussion again. "On the assumption the ice cream hooker is right; we have to get the money out of the damn building on top of everything else. Raymond must be slipping if he let this hooker see where he's keeping his stash. He has to be in full paranoid mode at this point." I look around the table, hoping for some constructive input on this mess.

Eric leans forward, "I think perhaps Raymond has taken to quality checking his product a little too often. He's become afraid of the wrong things. Simple things are slipping by him. You'd think his second would step up. Of course, this might be him trying to take over and probably get the poor bastard killed." Eric always seems to be able to summarize the big picture.

"Are we still going to bring down the building?" Cane asks, not sure if this new information changes things.

I nod and wait for someone else to speak.

Eric doesn't disappoint me. "I agree; we should keep to our original plans. Having to pick up any cash may require a few more men, guns and a little bit of extra planning, but the result is the same."

Cane nods at Eric and Jack chuckles to himself. I lean back in my chair waiting for Max to call with an update. In the meantime I'm trying to figure out how much money this fool could have and how much additional risk this new twist is going to cause. The guys switch gears, so they can figure out what it will take to get an unknown amount of money out and how many additional men we will need. I'm only vaguely paying attention. Jack taps his lighter on the table. I shake off the haze and look at him. He nods towards the table. I look at everyone and it appears I have been asked for my approval. "If Jack's good, then I'm good," I answer. They all nod in agreement.

Jack's phone rings. "Max what'd you get?" He puts the call on speaker.

"The hooker has some very specific details and I believe her. She says it's a large stand-alone safe in the middle of one of the bedrooms in Raymond's suite on the top floor. It will probably take two people to haul the cash out and perhaps two more as an escort."

Jack nods, agreeing with Max's assessment. "Okay, Max, pay her and come on back."

"Done." The connection is broken.

"Jack, call Max back," I tell him. He hits the speed dial and we wait for Max to pick up.

"Yep?" he says as soon as the line opens.

"Max do you still have the hooker with you?"

"Yes, Ma'am."

"See if you can get a head count and any other tactical info from her. We'll need it if we want to get away with this."

"On it," Max answers.

I look at Jack.

"What?" He asks.

"When was the last time you cracked a safe?"

Jack rubs his beard with both hands. "Shit, I thought we would just blow it open."

I throw a pen at him. "Good lord! I suppose we may not have a choice. This seems like a lot of unstable moving pieces to deal with and *now* we have to blow a damn safe too."

"I can open the safe," Cane says.

I turn to him not bothering to hide my surprise. "You can fight, you blow things up and now you're telling me you can crack a safe."

He taps the side of his head, "Not a just target."

"Show off," is all Jack has to say.

I laugh and push Jack's chair. "Well shit, we've solved the latest crisis. Let's keep moving things forward."

Cane and Eric continue to discuss how best to bring down the building. The rest of the guys are running different scenarios. They must approximate how many people are in the building and the presumed weight of the money and various weapons.

Jack's phone beeps and he reads the incoming text. "Max is on his way back and he says the girl claims she saw at least ten men. They were mostly in the stairwell going up to Raymond's suite. She only really spent time on the one floor. So, there could be others she didn't see. She also told him she was not the only *entertainment* working. To add to the shit stack, she is pretty sure most of the other entertainment is still in the building." Jack tosses his phone on the table in disgust.

I know exactly what he's thinking. We don't do collateral damage. Does it happen, yes, but we try very hard to make sure it doesn't.

"Listen up!" All discussions stop, and everyone gives me their full attention. "Raymond's guys are acceptable losses. With him dead it will only cause a damn vacuum. Then one of them will want to take their turn to stand on the top of crazy-mountain and wear the tin foil hat. However, the hookers are not acceptable losses. We need to get them out while we make sure the other morons go down with the building."

One of Eric's men speaks up.

"Why not make the hookers an offer better than the one they have." He looks at Eric and gets a nod to continue. "They come out and we go in. Worst case scenario, if Raymond's men hit the street we take them out. We can always drag their bodies back in the building before Cane and the demo team bring it down. Then they go down with the ship and it doesn't matter how many holes are in them." He looks around to see if this floats with the rest of us.

I turn to Jack and he has a look on his face I recognize well. It tells me it's going to be messy, but it can be done.

"Make the call," I tell him.

Jack calls Max and tells him to turn around. He also tells him to get Kevin to help him find out how many hookers are still in the building. Max is also told to find out how much they are being paid and make the appropriate deal with each of them.

I catch Eric's gaze, "Send team three and four to back up Max. We need to make sure they get the girls out. Should any of Raymond's men follow them out give our guys the green light. Best case there will be less of them when the rest of us get on scene." Eric nods and gets on his phone.

With those two teams leaving shortly, I know we need to get packed up and get over to the building. "Cane, take however many men you require to pack the fireworks we'll need. Eric will get the trucks ready when he gets off the phone. Jack and I will meet you and your teams in the garage in thirty. Anyone not down there isn't only being left here, but will also be painfully unemployed."

Everyone nods and rises from the table. Cane turns to me before getting up and lays my asp on the table. I pick it up as I watch him walk out the door behind Eric.

"An interesting turn of events," Jack says in his conspiracy voice. It sounds exactly like his asshole voice.

SIX

I meet up with Jack at the elevators outside my flat and we go down to the garage together. It's always important to Jack we arrive together. He wants the guys to know we are on the same page.

The elevator doors open to a scene of controlled chaos. The men are being outfitted with their weapons and protective gear. There's a cart next to my truck and I can see it has everything Jack and I will need. We both changed into what Jack likes to refer to as our hunting clothes before we came down.

We don't wear anything too complicated, just compression tops and bottoms, with black tactical clothes over the top. We don't make the guys wear matching clothes. They're not dolls. We all wear black and we all must wear protective gear. Each of the guys needs to be comfortable and able to do their various assignments. Jack and I put on additional compression vests first. Our tech people designed them. They're not only for compression but they also contain cold packs to be activated should we get severely injured. The compression and cold can hopefully keep us from bleeding out; at least that's the theory.

Jack reaches for one of the bullet proof vests and realizes as he fastens the first few buckles it's mine. I look up from fastening my leg holster and Jack is pushing down the subtle puffiness of the vest. "Since your man boobs aren't filling it out, I think it's safe to say it's one of mine." I'm trying hard not to laugh.

Jack unbuckles it, pulls it off and hands it to me. I fasten it and of course it more than fits the way it should. We don't always take everything the cage has chosen for us, but they always know what we might need. I always take my Heckler and Koch .45 caliber. It's seen as a big gun for a woman, but I don't think the weapon cares if you have a vagina. With twelve rounds in the magazine, I can put more than a few sufficient sized holes in a few people. I place it in my thigh holster. I put the ASP Cane returned to me, in a side pocket and a couple of switch-blades in a pocket on the opposite side.

Jack likes guns, a lot. By the time he's outfitted I'm convinced we're going to need a trailer to bring along enough ammunition for all his toys. He's a lot like Rambo in the movies; he always seems to have an end-less supply of bullets.

"Dylan, I think we're done here."

The string bean, shaved head, and tattooed young man makes his way over to the truck and takes away the cart. When the doors to the main elevator open; Cane and Eric empty out along with some of Eric's team. The stairwell opens, and the rest of the guys make their way to the cage to get what they need.

We travel in your typical TV-movie convoy style. The trucks and cars vary depending on the job, but they're all the same color. The only difference being our motorcade is blue, not black. I like black, but when it comes to my vehicles I prefer a dark midnight blue. Different manufacturers have numerous names for the same color, but they all have one. If they don't, we don't buy their vehicles. Now of course we could have a car or truck painted, but it seems like extra work. There are rare occasions when we must have a vehicle the dealers can't deliver timely. Then we buy a neutral color and have the guys in the garage paint it.

Jack uses his annoying stadium whistle, to get everyone's attention. "Let's get moving," he says into the silence.

My truck is already running, thanks to my driver. I see out of the corner of my eye Cane is talking to Eric. They shake hands and part ways. I look down at my phone to make sure I don't have any additional updates from the guys in the field.

"Woman, finish your lipstick in the truck. We got things to do," comes Jack's voice from inside the truck.

Part of my brain is trying to figure out why his voice is not muffled. The other part of my brain is trying to figure out why and how my door is already open. I look to my right and see Cane holding the door handle. In a blink he has managed to get this close to me and open the door without me even noticing. I make sure not to let my surprise show on my face.

"And they say chivalry is dead," I nod to Cane and get in the truck. As he closes the door and steps to the door behind me I turn to Jack. "By the way fuck off; I stopped borrowing your lipstick years ago."

Jack snorts in response. Cane gets in behind me and closes the door.

"Cane, I thought you'd ride with Eric and the explosives?"

He puts his hand on my right shoulder, "No."

"Alright, Bryce what's on the menu today?" I start

poking around the music selection. I know Bryce has a set list for me and I know he hates when I play with the buttons. It's why I do it.

"Boss, please push the button with the little rugby ball." Bryce says in his nice calm *'I have to teach 5-year olds'* voice.

I laugh and hit the scroll button one more time because I can. I wait for the screen to go back to the home display and find the rugby ball icon as instructed. I push it and out of the speakers I hear *Halestorm. Bryce is my hero.*

I point towards the giant doors and Bryce opens them. Our caravan starts to weave its way through the city, heading downtown.

We don't travel the entire way in a government style pack. The individual drivers have their own route around the city. I don't care what road they take as long as they get to their position on time. I realize how odd it may sound, but it works, and in our case, it's a lot safer.

The music in the truck cuts off as the voices of the team leaders start to echo through the truck. Each one checks in and lets us know they're in position. Our guys who will be joining us from the roof have made their way up the fire escape of the building directly across from our target. They came up with the idea of using the Freemont Street Experience as cover as well as a bridge to the roof of the old Binion place. My guys just aren't dangerous pretty faces. They're also smart as hell.

Bryce pulls into the alley and lets the other teams know we're ready. I go to grab the handle and as I do the door opens. Once again Cane has beaten me to the punch. As I step out our backup pulls into the other end of the alley, so the two vehicles are nose to nose. Colin the driver of the other truck and Bryce grab the collapsing ladders we brought along. They set them up in the bed of the designated truck.

Jack and I make our way to the back of the truck. He steps up onto the tire and gets into the back. I grab the tailgate and follow behind him. Cane and the two guys from Colin's truck are waiting for us to make our way up the ladders so they can follow us. In the interim they're watching both ends of the alley and the windows above us to make sure we have no uninvited guests.

Jack reaches the window first. He checks in with the guys on the ground to make sure the entertainment has been cleared from the building. It only takes a moment for him to get confirmation we are clear to enter. He lets the other teams know we're ready to break the glass.

Jack counts to three and we hear the other teams breach the ground floor and the roof of the building. The thinking is while everyone is headed down to deal with the guys on the ground floor, the team on the roof can get started with the explosives. Not to mention we can slip in behind them, get the money and get out without anyone knowing we were there.

The demolition team lets us know they've made entry from the roof and are starting to lay the charges. Since we want to collapse this mess around them; we are more concerned with the building folding in rather than down. Once we're all through the window the ladders are collapsed into the bed of the trucks. The trucks pull away to wait in their retrieval positions.

The one thing you can always rely on is drug

dealers will always have the instinct to protect their product. We had no doubt they would swarm toward the lowers floors since it's where all the selling was taking place. Good news for us, it leaves the upper floors virtually empty.

Jack takes the lead and Mack, one of our extra guns, follows him. Jim, the other gun follows them, but his job is to find the room with the safe and clear it. Cane and I are waiting for any new information from the teams as they continue their work. I can hear Jack and Mack start to yell 'Clear' as they make their way through the very large suite.

Jim calls out he has found the safe in the middle of a bedroom on the south side of the suite. Cane and I make our way to the room since it's one of the main reasons we came on this scavenger hunt. We get to the room and it's a disaster much like the rest of the suite. The room is void of furniture except for the safe. It's almost like the safe was a religious idol. I have an uneasy feeling, but I think it probably has more to do with this crappy building and all the ick, rather than anything really being wrong. Jim, having completed his primary assignment, leaves us to catch up with Jack.

The safe is nothing very space age. In truth it's rather old school. I start to wonder if maybe the feeling I'm getting has to do with the fact Cane may be good with 'hacking' safes, not necessarily cracking an old school one. Raymond was not lax with his choice, no matter the appearance. Most of the old school safe guys are out of the business nowadays. Even those who still do an occasional job are extremely hard to find. A lot of the young guys will not even take a job with an ancient beast like this.

I keep looking around the room trying to shake this nagging feeling of unease. Cane has disappeared from my line of sight. After not much of a search I find him on his knees in front of the three-dial behemoth. It almost appears as if he's going to crack it by touch. He's going to have to be very good because with the amount of noise coming from above and below us there's no way he's going to be able to hear the tumblers.

The gun fire and the screaming are a bit much, but at least I know our guys are doing their jobs. I'm standing in the doorway keeping watch and it already feels like we've been in this damn room for hours.

Jack circles back into the suite. "How we doin'?" He lights up one of his stinky foreign cigarettes.

"I have no idea. He hasn't asked for help or thrown a tantrum so I'm going to say we're doing fine."

Jack lightly bangs his head against the door jam. Apparently, it wasn't the answer he was looking for.

I walk away from him and stand behind Cane. The safe is covered in what I can only describe as gibberish. With all the markings on the safe door I'm not sure if he's making any head way or if he's trying some curse to open the damn thing. I lean over into his ear, "Are you trying to hex it open or is there a method in there somewhere?" I wave my hand at the hieroglyphics.

Cane looks up, winks at me and goes back to work. Two of the dials have a face with X's for eyes scrawled next to them. I'm assuming it means he's cracked them. I make my way back to the Jack. He still has his head resting on the door jam.

"It looks like he's on the last dial," I tell Jack.

Jack nods and taps his ear piece. He tells me he's going to go and check in with the other two guys walking our floor.

I'm passively listening to the teams check in. So far, we have no serious injuries. It also sounds like the pyro guys are almost done.

"Oy!"

I turn to the sound of Cane's voice and there he is standing in front of the now open safe and grinning like it's Christmas morning.

I quickly join him, and we look inside. The only thing I can think to say is, "Well shit!"

On every single shelf there are large stacks of cash. I push my throat mic to let Jack know what we've found. Cane and I quickly open the bags we brought with us and start to load the cash. It doesn't take long, and I let Jack know we're almost done. I then hear Jack giving directions to the pickup drivers as well as the demolition team.

Cane shoulders his bag. I squat and lift the bag across my body like a messenger bag and start to make my way around the safe's large door, following Cane to the exit.

I hear splintering wood to my right and out of the closet bursts someone with a sawed off shot gun. I lunge just forward enough to push Cane through the doorway and fall back towards the safe door. Simultaneously I hear the shot-gun go off. I feel a searing pain in my shoulder and neck. It sounds like a damn cannon going off even with all the other noise in the building. I can feel a wet warm river start to make its way down my arm. I can just start to make out a pool of what I'm assuming is blood forming around my boots.

The blast from the weapon has caused on overwhelming ringing in my ears. I can barely hear Cane's voice and I can see he isn't too far away from me. I squeeze my eyes and focus on the voices in my earpiece. I pull out my HK and try to peak around the safe to see if I can get a clean shot at who or whatever popped out of the closet.

Cane is yelling, calmly, if it's possible. "She's been hit! Some fucker was hiding in the closet. Jack, come get this damn bag so I can get her out."

I do my best to again shake off the ringing. I collect myself and cut off his request "Cane, take my bag. Get the money to the truck, Jack will get me out."

My first thought is to get Cane out of the room. His focus is drifting from the job. It's not like I don't trust Cane to get me out but there's a bigger picture here. I need Raymond dead with his head on a damn pike in my office. No one life is more important than the whole, no one's. The crazy fucker who popped out of the closet is yelling something, but I can't understand a damn word he's saying. It sounds like someone stole his bunny, could be money, but I would bet all the money in my bag this fucker is yelling about his bunny. The shotgun goes off again, but the guy doesn't seem to be shooting at anything or anyone. I can almost hear Cane cussing near the door. I can't see him around the large safe door, but I know he's still in the suite.

I do my best to kick my bag of cash towards the doorway. "Cane, take the bag and get your ass down to the trucks!"

The shotgun goes off again and the window to my left breaks.

"Keep your head down I'm on my way!" I hear Jack's calm voice come over my earpiece.

I hear two quick blasts and I feel a thud I'm assuming is a body hitting the floor. The next thing I know Cane is next to me and he has a look on his face somewhere between white hot anger and complete focus. He takes off his bullet proof vest and pulls his shirt off. It seems like a strange thing to notice, but I seem to be focusing on the fact he isn't wearing a compression vest. Of course, I also notice he's ridiculously fit. I'm going to file this away as a symptom of blood loss.

As he pulls a roll of duct tape from one of his cargo pants pockets, I pull the cords releasing the cold packs. He tears his shirt in half and wraps part of it around my shoulder. He takes the other part of the shirt and wads it into a ball. He tears off a strip of tape and presses it hard against my neck. He secures a couple of pieces of tape to my back and chest to hold the neck compress in place.

Cane stands and walks back around the safe dragging the bag I tried to kick towards him. He squats down next to me, "Let's get the fuck out of here before anymore Crack-in-the-boxes pop out." I laugh as best I can and lean heavily on him as he helps me to my feet.

I turn around and Jack is making sure the guy from the closet it dead by putting two more holes in his head. We get to the doorway and Jack joins us. Coming toward us from the hallway are the two guys who came in with us. Jack tries to take me from Cane, but Cane moves us forward without acknowledging him. Jack yells for Mack and Jim to grab the bags. We all make our way down the stairs as he gives the order to the pyro guys to do their thing. We make it down the stairs and Cane kicks the push bar on the door so hard it slams, and wedges open against the van waiting for us.

Cane steps up into the van and lifts me on his hip like a Siamese twin. He turns and sits on the bench with his leg up against the van wall. He sits me on the bench in front of him, so my bleeding shoulder is facing the center of the van. I can hear, over the earpiece, the demolition guys have set the timers and all our men, including the injured, have been cleared from the building.

Jerome is our most experienced doctor. It's good to see him in the van. He takes a knife from his boot to cut the vest straps and removes the make shift bandage Cane applied upstairs. He starts to do his thing and at the same time his assistant Caleb starts a line for blood and fluid on my uninjured arm. Cane starts to loosen the straps on the compression vest, but Jerome tells him the cold needs to stay in place until we get back to the buildings.

I hear Jerome tell Jack the shot must have hit the safe door. It sounds like he's saying the injuries are more shrapnel related rather than direct shotgun related. Before I drift off I hear him say, "Jack I don't know how much damage is in the neck, but I don't recommend stopping for any lights."

I don't really remember much else about the ride back to the buildings, but I have a feeling it was very quiet. When the van stops Jack slides the door open, so he and Caleb can jump out. In my peripheral haze I see Caleb pushing the gurney next to the open van door. I feel Cane rise behind me and I try to use the side of the van to pull myself up.

"Don't even try it," I hear him say. He squats next to me and lifts me from the bench to the gurney before Jack can get inside the van to assist. Jerome crawls out after us and begins to hook up a lot of expensive machines as one of his assistants covers me with a blanket.

Caleb and Jack start to push me quickly towards the waiting elevator when all hell seems to break loose behind us. "What the fuck is going on?" I ask Jack, grabbing his hand. Jack takes off and I motion for Caleb to turn the gurney, so I can get a better look.

What I see is Cane in a pushing match with another team member. The man throws a punch with his right arm, but Cane steps to his left and blocks the punch. Cane traps the man's right arm and I hear a snap as the elbow breaks. Cane follows with a left hook and the man goes down.

Jerome doesn't even turn to see what's going on; he's on the phone to the surgeons on call telling them what's headed their way. Jack reaches Cane, and with help from Eric, they pull him off the guy out on the garage floor.

I motion to Eric for him to bring Cane to me. I see him lean down to Cane's ear, Cane looks at me and I wave him over. Caleb is getting anxious and to be honest I'm using all the strength I possess to stay conscious.

Jack starts giving instructions to take the unconscious guy on the floor to our clinic.

Cane reaches the gurney and begins to help Caleb wheel it into the waiting elevator. "What was that all about?" I ask.

"He was the one who was supposed to have cleared the room we were in," he says with complete confidence, believing he did the right thing. "But he missed the asshole with the shotgun in the closet. Next time he fucks up like that I'll kill him."

I look up at Cane, as my eyes close and the sedation and blood loss takes over. I manage to place my hand on his before I pass out completely.

SEVEN

I come to and can hear only machines. I can, however, tell I'm not on the medical level. Part of me realizes this is probably a good thing. I look over and see Cane sleeping head down near my hand. It appears from the increased hair on his face, and the fact he has the same bloody clothes on, he hasn't gone very far. I look to the other side of the bed and see Jack asleep in a chair with his boots on my bed. If I felt better and had a gun, I would shoot him in the foot. I reach out trying not to tangle my IV connections and manage to push his boots off the bed.

He sits up only mildly startled and looks at me as if I'm the one who was rude. "Well hello. How nice of you to join us," he says in a low raspy voice as he stretches his arms over his head.

"I feel like I've been laying here forever. How long?"

"Only a day," Jack yawns and leans toward me.

I point towards the still sleeping Cane. "What's the story with him?"

"He hasn't left your side. He even went in to surgery with you and has been here ever since. The only time he's gotten up is when I'm here and then only for the bathroom. I don't think he's eaten in a while. I know Eric brought him water and a few meal bars, but not much else."

"So, what's the diagnosis, it must not be too bad if I'm in my flat and not down stairs." Jack looks at Cane and shakes his head a bit.

"Apparently there was more shrapnel from the safe than actual shot. The crazy guy must have hit the safe and you got the spray from it. The doc says nothing major was hit and he can correct any scars you don't like. He says he made the stitches nice and small. You'll need to be careful and take it slow for a week or so but, you should be good."

I shake my head the best I can and tell him to go get Eric and the doctor. He gets up and quietly leaves the room. I take a deep breath and tug at Cane's thumb which is curiously hanging on to my blanket. Cane wakes up a bit alarmed. He reaches down quickly for what I assume is the knife in his boot and then looks at me and the machines. I suppose he was checking for some sound or alert, something was wrong. He looks back at me and realizes I'm awake. He removes his hand from his boot and collects himself.

"So, I hear you've been with me since the elevator?"

He runs his hand over his face and smiles. I put my hand over his and squeeze the best I can. There's a knock at the door and I nod. Cane calls for whoever it is to enter. Jack and Eric make their way into the room.

"Hey Boss, glad to see you're awake."

"It's good to be awake. Did the building come down clean?" I ask Eric.

He looks at Jack, but says nothing.

Jack looks sheepish and finally says, "Let's talk about it while we eat."

"Fine, Eric, please take Cane to get some actual food, a shower, and some sleep." Cane looks at me as if to protest and I lift my hand to silence him. "I more than appreciate all you've done. We'll talk about it all later. Now you need to take care of yourself. You need to shower. You need to eat some real food. Most importantly you need to sleep. I want your phone off and I want you to sleep for at least six hours, if you sleep for twelve it would be even better."

Cane quickly realizes further discussion would be futile.

"Come on brother let's get you taken care of." Eric puts his hand on Cane's shoulder. Cane gets up and is visibly stiff from being in the chair so long.

"Eric", I call out. He turns toward me. "Make sure he eats." I give him a look he knows well. Eric winks at me and I know Cane will have no choice but to follow my instructions.

Jack brought food and drink with him. I also see the doctor is waiting his turn.

I wave at him. "Okay doc, let's hear it."

"All I have is good news. Everything should heal fine. As I told Jack, if any of the scars bother you, we can fix them." He talks while checking the bandages.

"Ok, so the question of the day is, when can I get out of this bed and how soon can I travel?"

The doctor puts out his hand and Jack reaches into his pocket. He pulls out a fifty-dollar bill and slaps it into the doctor's hand. I do my best not to smack them both. Sometimes I think Jack uses bets like this to give people bonuses.

"No shooting until next week, this includes real and

paper people. However, you can get up and travel tomorrow should you so desire. There is one stipulation. Wherever you go there needs to be someone to change your bandages." I nod to let him know I understand. The doctor shakes hands with Jack and leaves the room.

Jack puts the tray of food down and wheels the table over to the bed. He takes the lid off and the smell of cheese enchiladas fills the room.

"The woman is a mind reader," I tell Jack.

"I have no doubt," he pours himself some tea from the pot on the tray.

"So, get on with it. What happened?" I ask as I slowly start to eat.

Jack puts his cup down and folds his arms over chest. "Well, I can tell you the fire department is pissed, and the cops are not much happier. The building came down like it should. The inside caved leaving most of the external walls standing. The fire, however, got a bit out of control. From what we can tell, Raymond must have been storing chemicals of some kind, maybe he was running a meth lab, and when the fire reached whatever it was, things got pretty hairy." Jack reaches into his pocket. He takes a deep breath and lays a ring on my blanket. Raymond's ring.

I close my eyes and lean back on the pillows. "It's not the fuckers head, but I'll take it." I take a deep breath and look a Jack. "Okay, send the charity people to see them and make sure this gets cleaned up. Don't forget about the surrounding neighbors. Also check with the city to make sure they don't need anything else from us." I open my eyes and look at Jack, since he isn't saying anything.

"I'll take care of it." He pauses, "So... Should I call the airport?"

"Yes, I want to leave first thing in the morning." I start in on my food again and drain the large bottle of water.

Jack takes out his phone and starts to make the arrangements. He stands up and kisses me on the top of my head before he leaves me alone.

I spend the rest of the day watching TV and sitting on different pieces of furniture in my flat. Eric stops by and lets me know Cane is still asleep. I'm sure it had more to do with Donna dosing his food and less about him wanting to be asleep. Sometimes you must take the decision out of their hands. He'll be better for it in the end.

Jack comes by as the sun starts to go down to give me an update of the day's events and to let me know our charity people were able to make peace with the city officials and law enforcement. I was pretty sure it wasn't going to be an issue, but it's good to hear everything is resolved, especially since I will be leaving for a much needed break.

"What time do I leave tomorrow?"

Jack looks at his phone. "Looks like the pilot will have everything ready by eleven tomorrow morning. I spoke to Mana and he will be here to pick you up at ten-thirty."

I nod at him, knowing if he has talked to Mana I don't have anything to worry about, except maybe Cane.

I can't vanish on him because I have a feeling it has happened to him more than once. I need him to listen when I tell him he'll be staying here. I think perhaps meeting Mana may help. "Tell Mana I need him here at ten instead. I have a feeling telling Cane he's going to remain here is going to be a problem."

Jack shrugs and sends a text. He makes sure I don't need anything before he leaves again.

I use the intercom to ask Jacob to come up when he has time, so I can get packed. Thirty minutes after I call, he's in my closet with me, packing everything I will need for my trip. Jacob puts the bags next to the door and I bid him goodnight. I get about two steps away and hear a knock at the door. I open the door and find Eric standing there.

"What's going on?" I open the door wider to invite him in.

"Boss, I wanted to check with you about what you want Cane to work on while you're away. I was going to ask Jack, but you know he spends the time you're away at the cabin."

I laugh and offer him a seat at the big carved wood table currently covered with ideas for my new ink. I move the papers to the other end of the table and I offer him a beer which he happily accepts.

"I think perhaps you should tell me what *you* think since you'll be the one working with him while I'm gone, and Jack is busy fucking glamping."

Eric laughs and leans back in the chair. "I think maybe I should talk to him about his impulse control. His quick decisions could become a problem in the future. I mean at some point we'll need to question someone, and he may have already cut off their head."

I laugh out loud because I know he's right. "I think

it's as good a place as any to start, but keep in mind, I'll only be gone a week."

He grins, "Also, I think maybe I'll work with him at the range and get him more assimilated with how we do things here. We need some insight as to how he may react in other situations."

I give him the go ahead. We chat about some other things and he finishes his beer. I get up and walk him to the door. "Do me a favor; try to get some of his back story while I'm gone. I'm not asking you to report back to me. I really think he needs to tell someone."

"You got it, boss."

I shut the door and knock on it. My nightly cue to my security guys to lock the doors for the night.

I wake up to the smell of bacon and Jacob opening the drapes over the landscape windows near the ceiling. He knows a little light is fine, but if he's uncovering all the upper windows I suppose it's time to get up. I make my way to the bathroom to get ready. I'm all showered, dressed and Jacob is kind enough to change my bandages. I come out and breakfast is on the main table and of course Jack, the moocher, is already seated and eating.

"You better have left me some bacon you fucker," I sit down across from him.

"Jacob would poison me if I ate all your precious bacon," Jack mumbles over a mouth full of eggs.

Jacob drops off a tray of waffles and pancakes. Sometimes I think he simply cooks stuff he sees on TV.

"Jacob, are you expecting an army to join us?"

"No, Miss, but I was informed Mr. Wai would be joining us this morning." He says as he places the tray on the sideboard.

"You are correct. I suppose we're going to need more food. Mana can eat his weight in everything." I laugh and put more bacon on my plate.

The intercom on the table buzzes. I hit the button, "Yep," is all I say.

"Boss, Mana and Cane are both out here and it's a bit tense," is Craven's response.

I laugh, "Well I would hate for you to be scared. Send them both in, thanks."

"You got it, boss," is all I hear before the locks give way and Cane pushes through the door in front of Mana.

I assume the tension is coming from Cane since Mana couldn't give a crap about anything other than what he's being paid for.

"Please," I wave my arm at the empty chairs. "Take a seat everyone, there's plenty to eat."

Cane takes a seat next to me and Mana sits at the other end of the table. I think primarily because it's where most of the food is located.

"How are you feeling?" Cane asks.

"I'm good," I nod, "and by the time I come back next week, I'll be back to normal."

Cane has a look on his face of confusion mixed with a bit of anger I think. Then he asks, "Where are we going?"

I put my fork down and I know I must do this now. "*I'm* going to go and get some rest. *You* are staying here so you can learn more about what we do here. Mana is here to make sure I get where I'm going and to make sure I get back here safely."

Cane lets what I said sink in. He takes a deep breath, clenches his teeth a bit and nods his agreement.

This isn't what I expected, and I glance at Jack. He has a confused look on his face. I think we both thought this would be much more dramatic.

Mana hasn't said anything. He's a massive beast of a man. He stands six-eight and weighs in at a solid three-fifty. He's part island and part bear I think. He really lives by the Road House code of, be nice, until it is time to not be nice. There's a knock at the door and before I can say anything Jack yells for whoever it is to come in. Eric enters and tells me my transportation is ready.

"Jack, are you driving me to the airport?"

He gives me two thumbs up.

"Ok I'm gonna' change and we can go. Mana, would you be so kind as to take my bags with you when you go down to the garage?" I look at him and he's still eating, but one of his hands is raised with his thumb up.

I buzz Jacob to tell him we're done, and he can clean up whenever he likes. I change my shirt since I tend to use it like a napkin. I know, in all likelihood, there is bacon grease on it somewhere. I make my way to the main doors and Cane is standing there, I presume waiting to talk to me. I stand in front of him and wait for him to either open the door or say something.

Cane sighs; albeit quietly. "I accept Mana will take you wherever you're going and it's clear he's more than capable of taking care of things."

I wink at him and he opens the door.

I wave at the guys sitting at the desks as the elevator doors close. When we reach the garage level Jack is wrestling with Mana and Eric is leaning against the truck watching. Now I don't mean Jack and his old ass is trying to take Mana down. It's more like Mana has Jack in a hold and Jack's trying to escape without dying. Jack thinks it makes him look brave when in fact he looks like a ragdoll Mana likes to play with.

I always think of the old cartoon with the sheepdog and the duck, *'I will hug him and squeeze him and call him George'*. Eric sees me and taps Mana's giant arm. Mana let's go of Jack and if Jack's center of gravity was less than perfect he would have fallen on his face.

"I guess we're ready to go," Jack says as he straightens out his clothes.

Cane takes the bag from my shoulder and gets into the back seat. Jack gets in the driver's side with Eric behind him. Mana likes to sit in the very back of the SUV. He barely fits, but no one would ever tell him couldn't sit wherever he wants. Donna walks up to my side of the SUV and I power down the window. She hands me a Pyrex container holding what I know are her cheese enchiladas. Based on the size of the tray I know they're not only for me. I thank her and power up the window.

Jack hits the horn and the doors open. We pull out of the garage and into the sunlight.

We arrive at the executive airport where the plane is ready and waiting. I see Jack requested our Bombardier Global 5000 for this trip. It's the smallest of our fleet. This plane only seats thirteen or so comfortably. Since I'm only taking Mana with me and not an entire security detail, Jack of course made the right choice. He pulls up to the rolled-out carpet.

Eric and Cane get out, mostly so Mana can unfold from the back. Cane grabs my bags and makes his way onto the plane while Eric waits at the truck with Jack.

Cane exits the jet and takes the food dish from me and carries it on board.

Mana is quietly standing his post at the base of the stairs.

Cane exits the jet again and the pilot follows him down the stairs. He's an old friend of Jack's and he walks over to say hello.

Cane comes to stand in front of me. "The inside of the plane looks like you," he says in a low whisper.

I look at him with a grin and a question on my face. I decide against asking the question and I lean in, "Don't kill or damage any more employees while I'm gone."

He nods as I step away from him.

I look at my escort. "Okay, Mana, let's get the hell out of here."

The pilot shakes hands with Jack and Eric. He makes his way back on to the plane and into the cockpit. I follow him, and Mana brings up the rear closing the cabin door behind him.

EIGHT

We touch down and I notice Jack and Cane waiting by the truck. I'm a bit tanner, mostly healed, and back to zero. I stare out the window as the jet taxis to a stop. They both look like they may have come from a fancy client meeting. Jack appears to have on new jeans and clean boots, while Cane is wearing obsidian dress slacks with a French cuff blue striped dress shirt, sans a tie. He has the sleeves rolled half way up his forearms.

I may have to speak to Donna; Cane appears to be stressing the limits of the fabric of his new attire. Of course, she does like to make sure the suits the guys wear look like a second skin. In Cane's case she gets a big shiny gold star and maybe a raise.

Mana lowers the stairs and Cane pushes off the truck. He meets Mana at the bottom of the stairs, shakes his hand and collects my bags. I exit the jet and say goodbye and safe travels to Mana. He comes with the jet, so he'll return to the happy place. Jack waves at the pilot and I turn to find Cane holding the truck door open for me. I get in and he takes the seat behind me. He places his hand on my shoulder and sits back in his seat.

I look over at Jack and ask. "Did you go camping while I was gone?"

Jack shakes his head, "No, a call came in two days

after you left. Eric and I have been working on it ever since."

"I know you didn't get all dressed up for me. Did you have a meeting before picking me up?"

Jack laughs, "No, Donna wanted to fit him for some proper fancy dress clothes and I happened to be with him when he was summoned. She made me try on some new stuff and we didn't have time to change."

I turn around in my seat and look at Cane. I really must admit he is wearing the hell out of his new clothes. I wink at him, turn back around in my seat and tell Jack to fill me in.

As it turns out some of our charity efforts has helped the local PD to clear a back log of DNA kits related to unsolved rape cases. This delay in justice is something I find inexcusable, but sadly it seems to happen everywhere. So, we help when law enforcement reaches out to us. It turns out a handful of the cases have been linked to one man. The issue, it turns out, is all but one of his most violent cases has exceeded the statute of limitations.

Jack says the bad guy doesn't seem to have a type or even a *gender* when it comes to his victims. This sadly only means there are likely more people out there who will never come forward. The current victim's case is about to run out of time, and the victim is still in a coma. It turns out she is the sister of a guy who is close to one of the members of the local SWAT team. The SWAT officer placed a call to Jack to ask if we could do anything.

Jack tells me the officer was mainly looking for information, things they can't get a hold of because procedure and the law dictate what they can and cannot do. We're more...*flexible*. Jack informed him he would get things started and when I returned I would make the call as to how much we could do. This was all crap of course because Jack knows *exactly* what I would say.

As we pull up to the building Jack hits the horn and the doors to the garage open. Kyle and Simon are waiting for us.

"I'm going to go up and shower. Give me forty-five minutes and I'll meet everyone in my office."

All Jack says is "Yep."

I turn to get my bags and Cane is already standing at the open elevator with my bags in hand. I step on the elevator; Cane follows, he slides his access card and pushes the button for my floor. When the doors open I hear the locks on my flat release. I say hello to the guys at the desks. They nod and say it's nice to have me back. My flat is as it should be, cool and clean. On the corner table on the way to my bedroom Jacob has placed a bottle of water. I really need to give him a raise, or a vacation or an island.

"Where would you like these?" Cane asks.

I turn and look at him. "Leave them there next to the door. Jacob will be in to collect them shortly I'm sure. He'll take everything and clean it and put it away himself. If I tried to do it, he'd explode."

Cane laughs and puts the bags where I indicated.

"Does Jack have you on the account he was talking about?" I ask.

"He does, I'm working on tracking."

I take a drink of the water, "Ok, I'll see you in there."

He nods and makes his way to the door. "It's nice to have you back." Before I can respond he has closed the door and left the room.

I finish with my shower and find clean clothes set out in my dressing room. I get dressed, reach a presentable state and make my way through the flat down to my office. As I open the doors I can hear more than a few voices. It appears like they're planning an invasion rather than tracking one piece of shit who needs to be put down.

"Hello gentlemen. Eric, how about giving me the short version of this mess."

He nods and begins his narrative. "Using the DNA, we were able to locate a relative serving time in Folsom. In addition, we've managed to find out this guy has three brothers and one of these shining examples of filth is who we're looking for. Good news for us, they all enjoy being guests of the penal system."

Eric goes on to tell me Cane has managed to track the most likely candidate to an old mining claim about an hour out of town. The others have been tracked down and they're nothing more than petty thieves. They seem to lack interest in human contact given their choice of crimes. This makes them unlikely to be our rapist.

"Cane, what makes you think the mountain man is our guy?" I ask.

Cane's answer was concise. "He has a look about him."

"Jack, we should send a team up there to check this guy out."

Jack nods and jabs his thumb at Eric and then at me. Eric laughs and unrolls a large topographical map onto the conference table. "Cane and I put together a team. We have two snipers, their spotters and four trackers. The trackers are camping on either side of this guy, but only one of them has encountered him. One of our trackers, Steve, says even with all the lowlifes and things he's seen; this guy gives him the creeps."

I lean over the table, so I can see the map and all the points the guys have marked. Cane looks at me and points to some purple marks on the map.

"These are places where other guys we may want to look at are hold up; there's some homesteader and hermit types up there. We think the creepy guy is either helping them, or leading them, or is their link to the city. Sadly, I think we need to take him off the mountain alive."

I look at Jack. "Well, shit. Are we going up the mountain or can the teams up there bring him down without frightening the other crazies?"

Eric takes out his phone and sends a text. In less than two minutes he answers my question. "Boss, the guys up there can bring him in as soon as the sun goes down." He looks at me for direction.

"Go ahead. It sounds like I could have stayed away for another week. You guys have this well under control."

Cane leans over. "I think ten days was plenty long enough."

Jack almost chokes trying not to laugh.

Eric starts to make the necessary calls to set their plan in motion. He and the rest of the guys leave to finish things up.

While I get up and take a seat behind my desk. Jack and Cane take seats across from me.

"So how was the island?" Jack asks as he puts some of his nasty chew in his cheek.

"It was mind-clearing, as always. I don't know why you ask. You know you're not going to get any details."

"I know," he says. "But it never hurts to ask."

"It might hurt if I punch you in the eye."

There's a knock at the door and Cane stands with his hand on his newly approved weapon. This might take some getting used to.

"Come in," I yell.

Eric walks in taking in Cane's demeanor, "Careful brother. Boss, the guys on the mountain are set and their spotters are anxious to come down. Apparently, the shooters are committed."

I laugh because I know its code for they all need a bath. "Sounds good, are we going to have eyes on this?"

Eric nods. "Cane, you wanna' come and give me a hand with the final details?"

He turns to me and I give him the slightest of nods. He winks and follows Eric out.

Eric stops before leaving my office, "I'll call as soon as we have video and audio." I wave at him as I start to look through the messages left for me by Jacob.

"Jack?"

"Yep," he says spitting into his bottle.

"Ten days ago, we were looking at a file with a politician and a goat, if I remember right. What happened?" Before he can answer I continue, "Also what happened with the fat smelly guy who was in our lobby?"

Jack looks at me and smiles, "Well I shot the politician and we set the goat free. I could give you all the details if you like, but the short version is easier."

I hold my hand to stop him from telling any more of what I'm sure would be mostly fantasy. "And smelly guy?"

"Well as it turns out the smelly guy's wife *was* in one of our apartments. She saw him being dragged out of the building, so she took it upon herself to go to the police and press charges."

"Who got fired for smelly guy making it into this building?" I throw away some of the messages.

"Not one of ours, it turns out smelly has a brother who works pushing papers for a local ambulance company. I brought this to the owner's attention and they have taken care of the problem internally."

I nod but add, "He still got all the way into the main lobby. Someone dropped the ball."

Jack looks at me, "I'll have Kevin look at the video from your point of view."

"Works for me."

Jacob enters the office through one of the sliding panels as if he were made of smoke. "Miss, they are ready for you both in the video room," he says.

Jack almost jumps out of his skin at Jacob's sudden appearance. "Fuck, Alex, get him a damn bell!"

I rise from my chair, but only barely because I can't stop laughing. I know Jacob sneaks in on purpose and it's funny every damn time.

As we leave the room I turn back to Jacob, "Please, get me the politician-goat file Jack took care of while I was gone." He simply nods, and I know the file will be there when I return. I really don't believe Jack shot the politician, but I'm sure there was some world-class Karma that they came up with to take down said fat cat.

When Jack and I get to the giant media room there are more people in the room than I thought there would be.

"Are we overlapping into the porn viewing hours?" I ask, as we enter the room. The space goes quiet and they all turn to look at me. They don't know what to say, but I can tell none of them want to leave.

"So, what the fuck are you all doing in here?" asks Jack, to no one in particular. A random voice from the bunch says something about wanting to see if these guys can bring the mountain man down without having to kill him. "Okay, well this isn't some peep show you screws. Anyone who isn't directly working this, grab a seat in the back."

I take another quick look around the room and nudge Jack. "Where's Joker?"

Jack points at the screens. "He's one of the long guns on the mountain."

"Kevin, turn the audio up, please." Kevin does as I ask, and the guys sit quietly except for one. I notice he's chatting to the man next to him. I put his disrespect to the side for now and try to concentrate on the audio and video display. Jack and I stand in front of the big screen with Eric and Cane behind us.

"Boss the sound is up. I'm waiting for something other than bug sounds to register." Kevin says as he continues to move the various buttons and switches in front of him. There's nothing on the screen, but I can now hear the faint sound of footsteps over the dry ground, but still nothing else of real significance.

A green hue comes over the screen. This tells us

whoever's point of view we are watching has turned on their night vision. It's not long until the person wearing the goggles is reaching out to take the shoulder of a man who is already crouching by the entrance of what looks like an old mine. The two men make their way into the shaft. There's clear evidence someone is living there, and they don't want unannounced company.

Proof of this is the remedial but effective can traps near the entrance, but the guys take care of those easy enough. The man with no green hue finds some very ominous explosives after the first turn in the shaft and those are also dealt with without issue. The man with the green hue takes the time to give the now disarmed explosives the middle finger. The sound of pots clinking, and a soft song comes over the speakers. The guys take positions on either side of the turn where we can see a dim light coming from what I would assume is a lantern or two.

"I got a dollar says they throw an FB around the corner," says a voice from the back of the room.

"Who said that?" I ask without turning around.

"Name is Conner, research and data mining." I hear the voice say.

An analysis geek, I really do hate people sometimes. "Stand up, Conner." I turn around. "Let's have a look at someone who is stupid enough to interrupt this operation."

He stands up, I think. He looks to be only about five-five with a closely shaved head and he also appears to be puffing out his chest.

"Well come down here let's have a closer look at

you." As he makes his way past the other men he elbows them as if to say, *hey look at me I'm moving up in the world*. I do note the other men don't acknowledge him. He stands in front of me with his head cocked slightly with his hands clasped in front of him. I'm sure I'm supposed to be impressed.

I'm counting to seven in my head. Before I can finish Cane asks him what FB stands for.

Conner doesn't even look at Cane. "It means flash-bang. Perhaps the person watching the boss's back should know the basics."

Before Cane can respond I ask Conner, "Who trained you?"

He cocks his head to the other side, "Kranston."

My response is terse with a hint of threat. "He doesn't work here anymore."

"Yeah, I know. He took a position with another firm. I was thinking about joining him, but I think I can move up the ladder faster here, if you know what I mean." He winks at me.

Before I can even contemplate all the horrible things I'm going to do to this ass hat, Cane has moved around me and has punched him right on the button. The mouthy homunculus is now laying on the floor out cold.

I turn to Cane, "What do you call that move?"

Cane puts his boot on Conner's neck. "I call it unconscious jack off." He motions back to the screen, "I don't think we missed anything."

I look over at Jack and he only nods at me. He knows we need to clean house and probably should've done it as soon as we removed Kranston from the property.

The screen has now been split into four equal parts. Two have green hues and appear to be standing at the opening of the mine. The other two are still standing around the bend in the mine shaft, from what I can only assume is the target. I have no idea what the plan is, and Jack seems to be a bit tense. However, it appears the on-scene guys have things under control.

The sound of men's voices comes over the speakers and two men appear on the screen. They're sitting across from each other on camping chairs.

"The guy on the chair, on the right, is Clark," Jack says.

The greenish figure on the right was, in fact, one of our best penetration assets, Clark. Even through night vision goggles he looked like a homeless guy with his long hair and beard. He'd been an Army Ranger Captain and then got attached to some secret squirrel DoD operations. And, believe it or not, when he wasn't doing ops in third-world shit holes he was doing…wait for it, little theatre. The guy could kill you three different ways with his bare hands while reciting any soliloquy from Richard the III. His acting and operational skills made him the go-to guy when we needed a homeless person on the street to watch a building or suspect, or a crash pad or hobo camp.

When we needed someone to infiltrate a business or financial op we used Collin, our token New Zealander. He'd been a policeman in Christchurch, working fraud and financial crimes. Although he didn't have the military background a lot of our team members did, he'd played semi-pro Rugby and was tough enough. Eric got him trained up in small arms and in close combat with Krav Maga and Russian Spetsnaz Sistema styles. He was tall and good looking with jet black hair and blue eyes. And there wasn't a woman admin assistant/gatekeeper that could keep him out of her boss' office once he turned on the Kiwi charm and accent.

But now it was Clark, looking like a ZZ Top wanna-be in the cave, working our suspect.

I hear a gurgling sound and I remember Conner is still on the floor. Cane takes it upon himself to take a bit of a standing punt at the fool's head. There is a slight spray of blood from his nose and Conner is out again.

I look up in time to see the target has offered Clark something to drink and Clark has in kind offered a bit of something from a flask from inside his jacket. The target gladly accepts. Once the target takes his first drink Clark touches his watch and a timer appears on the big screen. They begin to chat again for what seems like forever

I shake my head. The target continues to drink, and the two men continue to talk. At the two-minute mark on the screen the target literally falls off the camping chair he had been perched on. There's a whistle from Clark and the rest of the team enters the space. The screen now shows the target lying on the ground with his cup rolling away from his hand.

The men at the opening of the mine begin to give us details over their headsets.

"Kevin, we are ready to get the hell out of here. Tell the bosses." Kevin looks over at us and I wave him on.

"You got it brother. The cage is ready back here. Bring in the catch," Kevin responds.

The three men in the shaft stuff the target into a

giant duffle bag. The largest of the three gives his weapon to one of the others and lifts the bag onto his shoulder like a sack of grain. They join the men waiting at the entrance and they start to make their way down the mountain. Jack nods at Kevin and the screens go blank. Kevin continues to talk to the men on the mountain as the men behind us start making their way out of the room.

"Eric, get some guys to put this idiot into a cage until I figure out what I want to do with him."

Eric nodes, "Yes, Ma'am."

I point to Conner bleeding and still unconscious on the floor.

Cane is nice enough to take his boot off Connor's neck, so the guys can pick up his limp, slightly bleeding form.

I turn to Cane, "Well at least you didn't kill him. However, Donna may kill *you*."

He looks at me confused and I point to his white cuff where there's a bit of Connor's blood. "The shirt is at least a two hundred dollar, custom made Egyptian cotton. She's going to be a bit bent you got blood on it."

"I think if I wait to take it off in front of her while I explain what happened she may not get as mad." Cane grins.

Jack starts to laugh because he can't help it and I tell Cane it sounds like one of Jack's plans.

Cane waves his hand to usher myself and Jack out of the room.

I leave the rest of the details to Eric; he's more than capable of wrapping things up. We make our way back up to my office so Jack and I can talk about what to do with Kranston's minions. Before I sit down I turn to

Cane and hand him the file on my desk with the details about the politician. I want to find out what he would have done with the job if it had been assigned to him. Every situation here is a chance to learn.

"I want you to read this over and give a briefing in the morning."

He nods and takes the file.

"I also need you to go down and without killing him or breaking anything else, find out who the ass hat thinks he is."

He seems to get the point. "I'll check in later." He leaves the room and quietly shuts the door.

NINE

"Well old man, what the fuck are we going to do about this colossus cock up?" I plop down on the leather couch across from Jack.

Jack rubs his hands over his face and scratches his beard as he contemplates how to answer my question. "Shit! We got so wrapped up in the Raymond thing. Things went downhill fast when you got hit and then you went to your happy place to do the dance with no pants. To complicate things there was no real drama after Kranston was removed from the picture. No acting up of the staff, nothing. We've never had to clean house like this before. It turns out the bastard really *was* a fucking tumor: himself, the Doc, Conner." He sighs and looks directly at me. "This was my screw up and I'll take care of it."

"First of all, whatever dance may or may not have happened on the island is none of your concern. End of story. If you bring it up again, you *will* need someone to take you to the medical floor. Secondly, there's no fault here. We clearly placed our confidence in the wrong place when it came to Kranston. He walked a fine line and sadly it attracted a certain kind of people. It looks to me like it was maybe one bad apple and a couple of his sycophants. The rest of the guys have gone back to business as usual. I don't want to throw our organization into chaos with a mole hunt, at least for now. But keep a close watch over everything. We'll take care of this one moron and then do an overall assessment of all our teams. We can then determine if anyone else needs to go."

Jack slouches down in his old chair and I assume it means he's in agreement on both topics. We continue to chat until Jacob comes in with dinner for the two of us. Jacob also lets us know Cane has left the property.

I look at Jack and he gives me a look of confusion, clearly not knowing why Cane would leave or where he was going. I ask Jacob if anyone went with him. He says, not to his knowledge. I'm concerned, but not to the point I intend to send anyone after him. Instead I ask Jacob to have Kevin put a cell phone tracking report on my office screen. Jacob nods and lets himself out.

"Where do you think he went?" I ask.

"Don't have a clue," Jack replies. "As far as I can tell, he hasn't left the property other than with us since he was hired as a detailer."

Shortly after Jacob leaves, the main screen in my office comes to life with a map of the city. On it is a blinking red circle I assume is Cane. It appears he hasn't only left the property but has taken a car and is now on the south side of the city. Jack gets up and retrieves the remote from my desk. He enlarges the map, so we can get a better view on what the surrounding streets and buildings are. He appears to be parked at a storage facility. Well, *now* I'm a bit curious. Jack turns and looks at me and I shrug. I lean forward and hit the button on the intercom for Kevin.

"Yes, Boss," comes his voice out of the speaker.

"Can you get me any camera views of the storage facility Cane is currently visiting?"

"Give me a second I will see what I can do." We wait as he taps away at the keys on one of his many keyboards. "I got a visual for you. I will split the screen."

I thank him and disconnect.

Less than a minute later the screen divides and we can see Cane has parked next to one of the units. The door is rolled up and the car trunk is open. The picture is obviously not as clear as we would like it to be, but we can make out he's putting an armful of clothes into the trunk along with what looks like boxes of food.

I turn to Jack. "Do you think he was *living* in the unit before coming here?"

Jack takes a deep breath. "Do you want me or maybe Eric to talk to him?"

I shake my head. "No, let's leave him be. He's not hurting anyone and there's no need for us to be in his business. Let's have Eric remind him he has to check in with one of the three of us before he takes off."

Jack turns off the screen and sits back in his chair. "I think since he now has a place here inside the building, this won't happen again."

It's my turn to take a deep breath. We finish our dinner in silence.

Jacob comes back to pick up our dinner tray and lets us know the teams have returned from the mountain. We thank him and head downstairs to the basement. It's conveniently located two floors under the main garage. Now, anyone who has ever tried to dig a hole in Las Vegas will tell you it is stupid to have anything so far underground. With each level at over fifteen feet high it's not only far down, it is the only place on the property cold in the summer. This very bottom level is also where the detention area is located. It's far enough down no sound gets out. Not to mention we also could gas the floor without killing anyone else in any of the other buildings. Lastly, heat sensors and ground penetrating devices are rendered useless.

The doors open, and we make our way down the long, wide hallway to the secure area.

"Tommy, how are things going?" I ask as we approach the desk.

"Hey boss, everything is quiet as always." At the same moment a tirade of cuss words comes from one of the cages down the corridor.

I raise my eyebrow at him. He winks and turns in the direction of the noisy prisoner. "Boy! I already tol' you if you don't shut yer mouth I sho-nuff gonna' tape it shut and let them twins give you a cavity search."

The cussing quickly stops. Jack can't help himself; he bends over at the waist and starts to laugh. Tommy's heavy Alabama accent always cracks him up. I hear boots approaching behind us and I turn to see Cane. He has changed into his usual cargo pants and extremely well fitted t-shirt. He looks a bit surprised to see us.

"Cane." I nod at him as he approaches. "Tommy told us it's quiet down here, so I assume you haven't had a chance to visit with your new friend."

He nods, "I had to make a trip to my storage unit. It took longer than I thought it would. I'll get to work." I move out of his way and nod at Tommy as he opens the gate leading to the containment corridor.

Jack digs his phone out of his back pocket. "Eric, I need to you to get the interrogation team down here." He hangs up and nods.

I walk down to the cell where things seem to be a bit quieter than I thought they would be. When I take a gander into the cell I see Conner is on the floor of the cell. Cane is leaning against one of the walls his arms crossed over his chest and one of his legs bent at the knee with his boot on the wall.

I shake my head. "If you killed him already you don't get a treat."

I almost think he doesn't hear me. Then Cane slowly turns his head towards me. His eyes have gone almost ice blue and the chill over the space speeds up my spine. To say the least, I don't need to stick around. I would not say he was in a zone, but he sure as hell had flipped a switch. I raise an eyebrow at him. He turns his head back and I hear his neck crack. I shiver from the creepy sound as I walk away. Jack starts to walk towards me. I pick up the pace a bit and shake my head at him.

"He needs to be left alone for this."

Jack shrugs and turns around.

"Tommy let me know if it goes badly," I say as I reach the desk.

He looks down the hallway, nods and moves the view of Conner's cell to his main monitor. The elevator doors open, and Eric walks out followed by two of Jack's best interrogators. He has summoned them, I assume, to work on the mountain man. I leave these guys to Jack, they're his people and he speaks their language.

I wave to Eric to follow me and I motion down the hallway. "Don't stand there at the cell and watch Cane, but keep him from killing the fool for now."

Eric gives me a strange look as I pinch the bridge of my nose. "In all likelihood this tool will die at some point, but Cane needs to learn restraint, as you said before I left town. There will be times when we will need these people taken alive and kept alive until we get what we need from them. He can't keep killing folks because he feels he has the high ground."

The look on Eric's face changes as what I'm saying sinks in. He takes a seat next to Tommy at the desk. Tommy turns the monitor containing the Connor and Cane visual, so Eric can see it a bit better.

Jack whistles at me; I turn, and he motions for me to follow him. It looks like the crazy pokey people have a plan to get us some answers. I hope Jacob has the pressure washer on standby. As I catch up to Jack he stops in front of the large interrogation space. Inside I see the man who was on the mountain is laid out on the medical table. The setup looks like someone being executed by lethal injection. Jack's people, I have learned, may show you one thing and suddenly, a dragon appears and bites the detainee's head off. It's all very confusing by design. I always try to wait until I'm told what's going on or shown what's going on. I go with the assumption I'm better not knowing what's happening, or I could get eaten by the dragon.

Jack has the two people he always calls on for difficult jobs, a more dissimilar pair you would never meet. When we need answers sooner rather than later, Jack calls in these two. The tall skinny one, whose name I don't know, is whispering to Jack. The skinny one only talks to Jack or his partner, a large woman. Skinny guy looks like a pencil with black hair. From what Jack tells me, pencil-man is the technically savvy one of the pair. Jack walks back to me and tells me they have pumped the guy on the table full of the round lady's own mix. It serves as a kind of truth serum I'm assuming. The round lady bothers me the most of the pair because she looks like she could be someone's grandmother, or worse, the teapot lady from *Beauty and the Beast*. You would never suspect she is extremely gifted when it comes to chemical and drug concoctions. She looks more like the cookies and cake type.

I watch her as she places a set of virtual reality goggles on the mountain man. The goggles are hooked up to a computer set up in the corner of the room. Jack waves his hand and round lady pushes a button on the remote she has in her hand.

The giant white wall at the head of the table begins to show what I can only assume is the same thing being shown to the mountain man through the goggles. Jack leans over and explains the visuals will show the mountain man a story he will believe is happening to him. Apparently, we will also use this to get any information about the other creepy mountain people, so we can wrap this entire cluster up.

From what I can tell, the wall is showing a recreated scene of the rape and assault we have the most knowledge of. There's no sound in the room because Jack knows I wouldn't like it. However, the mountain man begins to talk as if he's there. I turn so I don't have to see any of the visuals. Jack walks up behind me as he sees me searching my pockets. He hands me a small plastic packet of ear plugs. I rip the packet open and stuff them so deep in my ears I may need the doc to pull them out later. Gladly now I can't hear a damn thing.

I can sense motion around the table. I glance over

my shoulder and see skinny injecting something into the IV bag hanging near the mountain man. Jack makes his way to the head of the table. I can only assume he has started the interrogation. I watch as Jack writes something on a notepad. I notice the visuals on the wall have changed, but I'm still not interested in looking. Round lady is standing next to Jack when he hands her something. She waddles over and hands me a note. The paper has Jack's scrawl on it. It says they have given this guy a paralytic. He can apparently feel and see everything but can no longer move. I always imagine the drug is what absolute fear feels like.

The note also says he is going to ask him about the other men on the mountain and his relationship to them. Of course, in my mind if he can't talk then Jack better freakin' know how to read minds. It is shit like this which makes me believe Jack is part super villain, but the kind you might have a drink or sex with.

Round lady has placed a cap of some kind on the guy's head and it of course has a bunch of creepy wires hanging out of it. This must be how they are going to turn his creepy thoughts into words. It could also be a brain sucking device, who the hell knows? Jack is motioning at me and I can see he wants me to take out my ear plugs. I comply and notice the room is mostly silent. The only things I can hear are the computer's faint hum, the interrogator's shoes tapping on the concrete floor as they go about their work and the beeping medical equipment monitoring our guest. It's more than a little unsettling.

After more than an hour Jack is still asking questions. The round lady motions to the monitor over the door. I can see Eric standing at the door covered in what

I can only assume is a lot of *not good* and waving at the camera. I motion to Jack letting him know I will take care of it. He waves and goes back to whatever brain scrambling crap he has planned. Round lady follows me over to the door, opens it and secures it behind me once I have stepped into the hallway.

"What happened?" I ask Eric because the look on his face and the blood covering most of his clothes tells me something has gone horribly wrong.

He motions to the elevator and I follow. As we step in I see him hit the button for the medical floor.

"Eric, if I have to ask you again, I will shoot you in the fucking knee."

He hangs his head and takes a deep breath, "Conner attacked Cane in the cell."

"What happened?" I ask again as I reach out for his arm.

He looks me in the eyes, "Conner bit Cane. He went right for his neck and then... Fuck! I'm not sure what happened. It looked like a horror film on the monitor. By the time I got back to the cell and Tommy opened it Conner was dead, Cane was covered in blood and I couldn't tell how badly he was injured. Boss, I'm sorry."

I grab his chin and force him to focus on me. "If we don't know the injuries then we don't know what to be worried about. We'll talk to the doc and then, if I have to shoot you at least we'll already be on the correct floor, so you can get treatment." He smiles slightly, and the elevator doors open to a scene of controlled chaos.

Since I know there should be nothing else going on now I'm a bit perplexed because there seems to be two areas of concentrated work going on. I would think the entire staff would be treating Cane.

"Eric, where's Connor?"

He tells me he was also brought to the medical floor.

"I thought you said he was dead."

Eric looks confused, "Shit. I mean, he must be. There's no fucking way he's still alive."

We are very careful not to walk too much in the copious amounts of blood smeared on the floor. I make my way over to the smaller group of medical staff and I push some of them to the side. "Is this the bastard who decided to chew on one of my men?"

The doctor trying to assess his wounds looks up at me and nods.

"Let him die." I walk to the other side of the cavernous space to check on Cane.

I could barely hear some of the staff behind me asking one another if I really meant for them to let the man on the table die. The doctor, having worked for us for a while, knows exactly what I meant. He directs his staff to fetch the cleaning crew and to find out if the other team needs any help.

Cane is in a larger triage space. His eyes are closed but he's sitting up. He remains still while the doctor is using staples to close the wound in his neck and shoulder.

"What in the fresh fucking hell happened in there?"

The doctor doesn't flinch. He's used to me bursting in and yelling, his nurse not so much. My abruptness startles her. She drops the clean bandages all over the floor and tips over a small table holding some sharp medical instruments.

The doctor simply shakes his head, "Marjorie please go and get more of whatever you spilled all over the floor. I need to fill Alex in on this man's condition."

Marjorie nods and takes the long way around the room. I'm assuming to keep her distance from me.

I look back at Cane and his eyes are now open and back to their gray blue color. The left is more open than the right. The doctor continues to staple as he begins to tell me about Cane's injuries.

"To be honest Alex, of the two of them his wounds are not too bad. It appears he took some of these to get closer to the other guy. He has these nasty chew marks down his neck to his shoulder and some nice gouges on his ribs as well as other parts of his upper body. The other one must have gotten in a lucky shot to get his eye to close." The doctor is very calm and continues to work.

"I assume you gave him a rabies shot," I ask.

The doctor chuckles, "Yes, Alex, I gave him all his shots to make sure there would be no infections."

The nurse returns with a new tray of instruments and more clean bandages. She fills a small bowl with saline I presume and starts to dab at the crusted blood on various parts of Cane's anatomy. I get annoyed very quickly.

"Marjorie is it?" I ask.

She looks up at me shocked when she realizes I am indeed talking to her. "Yes, Ma'am," is her shaky response.

I do my best to remain calm. "Marjorie, the first thing you need to learn is these boys are not frail or dainty. You need to do whatever needs to be done so you can care for them and complete your task."

I take a bandage from the tray, dunk it in the bowl and ring it out. I motion her to step back. I begin to firmly, but carefully wipe away the blood from the other side of Cane's neck. I look back at the nurse and get a confirming nod she understands what she needs to do. I step back, and she takes over.

The doctor stands up and calls over one of his interns and tells him to get Cane into a private room. He also tells him to go ahead and finish up the minor stitching. The doctor comes to stand with me at the end of the bed. I find my hand is resting on Cane's leg as the doctor talks to me.

"He has some pretty deep gashes from his shoulder to his neck. I can tell Conner was trying to get to all the major bleed points. Your boy had deep wounds under his arms and towards his groin."

I look at the doctor with not really shock, but disgust. Cane is covered to the waist with a sheet. I now notice what's left of his clothes sticking out of a bag on the floor in the corner of the room.

"How long will he need to be down here?" I try to contain my rage.

The doctor thinks about it for a minute and tells me Cane will need to stay for at least a day if not two. "Even when he's released he'll need to rest at least a week."

I feel Cane move his leg. I look up and he's trying to shake his head. I take a deep breath and ask the doctor if he can be moved up to his room and continue his care up there.

Doc considers for a moment, "If things don't get

worse overnight then tomorrow afternoon he can be moved. However, he will have to remain in a hospital bed with constant care."

Cane nods as if he believes he has a vote. I thank Doc and he calls for the nurse to follow him.

A couple of orderlies move Cane's bed and machines into a private room. Once they get everything situated the intern continues working on the upper body wounds. He leaves the room and returns with another suture tray. "Ma'am, do you mind if we switch sides? I need to work on the thigh gouges."

I look up at him and move to the other side of the bed. He lifts the sheet and folds it back so as not to expose any naked parts. Cane carefully turns his head toward the side I'm now on but remains silent.

"Is there a reason why you're not using staples there?" I motion towards the wound. I can see the gash is rather deep. The intern looks up and tells me the doctor felt because of the location stitches would be better to allow movement and healing. Not to mention given the area, staples can be irritating to his man junk. I nod, makes sense to me and I don't even have any dangling bits.

The sliding door opens and Jack steps in. "What the fuck is going on out there? It appears the prick is slowly dying on a table and the staff appear to be ignoring him."

I look at Jack. He looks around me at Cane and I can see understanding move across his face.

"Did Connor try to fucking eat him?" Jack leans over to look more closely at Cane's various wounds.

I tell Jack what the doctor told me, and he sits heavily down in the chair next to the door.

Jack leans over and puts his elbows on his knees, "Should I go out there and shoot him a few times? You know in the legs or something?"

I look at Cane and he grins a little. "No Jack, let the fucker die as slowly as possible," I say as I look back watching Cane close his good eye.

Jack sits back in the chair and looks at me as if he wants to say something but is not sure where to start.

"Spit it out old man," I stretch out my leg to kick his boot.

"I think we need to have a sit down with every employee from the landscapers to the head bean counter. We need to weed out anyone else who might be spinning along the same mind set as Kranston. We don't need any more of his groupies with their, 'I'll ask for forgiveness not permission' mindset. We can't function by putting out these fires one at a time."

I agree with him and tell him to set up the meetings. "We need to pull in everyone from the field unless they're in a position where it would cause an issue for a client. We need to start first thing in the morning."

Jack nods and pushes himself out of the chair. He leans over to kiss the top of my head and walks out the sliding door. I know he and Eric will start the ball rolling.

I hear Cane clear his throat. I look over at him and he points to the water container on the side table. I pour him a cup and find a straw in the bedside table to make things easier. I lean over the bed and hold the drink for him. The intern finishes up and covers Cane with the sheet. He asks if he needs anything else. Cane shakes his head and the intern leaves.

I ask him if he wants to watch TV and he nods the

best he can. I find the remote in the drawer under the TV. I turn it on but can't seem to find my DVR items. I push the speed dial for IT on the phone next to the bed.

"Kevin," a voice comes out of the speaker.

"Kevin, it's Alex, I can't get to my DVR stuff down here in Cane's hospital room, what the hell?"

I hear a sort of squeak, "On my way boss," before the phone disconnects.

I can hear Cane trying to laugh. I look over at him and raise my eyebrow. He has the nerve to stick out his tongue at me. In what I'm sure is record time I hear Kevin's voice outside the room. He knocks on the sliding door and I make a motion for him to come in.

"Hey, boss. I have a setup for you. All I need to do is plug it in." I looked at him and his face is beaded with sweat.

"Thanks for coming down so quickly, go ahead and do your thing." I look at Kevin's face. He's looking at Cane and starting to get a little green around the edges.

"Kevin, he's going to be fine." I snap my fingers in front of his face to bring him back.

"Yeah good, ok, yeah, I'll get this hooked up," he manages to stutter out. For guys like Kevin who look at the world and what we do via monitors it can be hard for them to see real life. Kevin plugs in some cables and hands me a new remote and lets me know I'm all set. He tells Cane not to die and almost runs face first into the sliding door as he hurries from the room.

I look back at Cane and he has a smirk on his face. I turn on the TV and the box Kevin brought down and like magic Cane and I can now watch one of the many Rugby Union games I've saved. I take my shoes off and curl up in the chair next to Cane's bed. We watch the game and I watch him fade in and out of sleep.

When I wake up, it's to the smell of antiseptic and, oddly, *bacon*. I open my eyes and try to un-kink my neck. I see Jacob standing in front of me holding a Ziploc bag with toothbrush, toothpaste, floss, mouthwash and new contact lenses. I also see two plates of food on Cane's tray table. Cane is awake and looks better than he did last night. I take the items from Jacob and I head into the bathroom to brush my teeth and change out my eyes,

I look back and tell Cane, "Don't eat my bacon."

He grins at me.

When I come out of the bathroom Jacob is gone. Cane mumbles with a mouth full of food telling me Jacob said to ring if we want more food. I give him an awkward salute. It's good to see he has his appetite. I open the sliding door to get some air circulating into the room. I also let the person at the desk know to send the doctor in when he's available.

Ten minutes later the doctor arrives and tells me we can move Cane up to his room at any time. I shake his hand and I ask him about Conner. He tells me he died from blood loss and probably some kind of cardiac episode. I nod my head and ask if he called Jack. He says he did and Jack has already sent guys down to pick up the body.

"Why did he bleed out, couldn't they stop it?" Cane asks.

I turn around, take my plate, and sit in the chair. "He bled out because I wasn't going to waste a bullet to put the fucker out of his misery." Cane looks at me and seems to understand what happened while he was being treated.

We finish up our breakfast in silence and eventually Jack makes an appearance.

"Hey boy, you look less like shit today. I mean better than the shit you looked like yesterday."

Cane smiles, "Well you look older and I didn't think it was even possible, you know, without being *dead*."

Jack smirks and I know there's a lot of relief behind it. "We have some nurses out here who volunteered to help you with a sponge bath, if you want one before we roll you and your electric bed upstairs."

Cane looks at Jack like he has three heads. "If you can help me onto the bench in the shower I can take care of myself."

Jack shrugs and looks at me. I step out of the room to make the arrangements to move Cane upstairs. I manage to finally locate the doctor in his office. I knock on the doorframe and he turns his head to look at me, not sure how long I've been standing there.

"Sorry, I was trying to finish Cane's report, so the upstairs team will have everything." He goes back to typing.

I nod and take a seat in front of his desk. "As soon as he's cleaned up he should be ready to move." I tell him.

I pinch the bridge of my nose and look across the desk. "I know you have the freedom to hire the best no matter what gender they are. However, as I was leaving Cane's room to find you, there were two nurses lingering outside his room. Jack informed us they volunteered to help Cane with his shower. This cannot go on in our environment."

The doctor looks at me and his expression is not a happy one.

"I will take care of it immediately," he says.

"How did he do it?" I ask.

The doctor looks at me. "Who?"

"Conner. How did a guy like Conner manage to inflict so much damage on a bad-ass like Cane. Shit, the kid who bags my groceries could take Conner."

Doc cocks his head and narrows his eyes.

"Okay, okay, so I don't buy groceries, Donna's minions do that."

Doc hands me a file. "Don't know how he got it down in detention, but your man Conner was juiced up on PCP. Here's the tox screen."

I look at the file. "No shit."

"Anxiety, panic, aggressively violent, feeling impervious to harm." Doc shakes his head, "Your Cane is a bad-ass, but Conner was something else entirely."

"Fuck! Thanks, doc." I nod, stand, and shake his hand.

When I get back to Cane's room the curtain is pulled back. I knock, and Jack looks out and opens the door. Cane is back in bed with a wet head. The remaining crusty blood and dirt from last night's mess has been washed away.

"The doc says you can be moved. He's finishing up the file, so the med team upstairs can monitor you." Cane seems relieved by the news.

Jack is standing in front of all the monitors rubbing

his stubble. "So, do I unplug him or the machines too?" He asks no one in particular.

I take the time to kick him in the ass and tell him if he touches anything, he will need a bed of his own.

Jack shakes Cane's hand and heads back upstairs.

A few minutes later, a two-man team enters the room with a list from the doctor. They brought some mobile monitoring equipment as well. They carefully unplug and reconnect all his various wires and make sure they have everything on the list marked off before they move to the next step. Once they confirm everything on the list is completed, they release the bed from its security locks on the floor. They slowly wheel everything to the large freight elevator on the other side of the medical floor.

As the door shuts, I can see at least one of the lingering nurses is being escorted into the doctor's office. I have complete confidence the doctor will take care of the situation.

I take the stairs, mostly because it will give me time alone to think about what happened and about how it could have been so much worse. I eventually join Cane in his room. He quietly asks me about his room. I can tell he's more than a little surprised to have found his room all rearranged. The furniture had been moved or cleared out completely to make sure there was more than enough space for the medical bed and his caretakers.

I push the pain killer button on the fancy drug machine. When I see it start to take effect I lean in and whisper to him, "Jack only *seems* like an asshole."

He tries to focus on me with his good eye, but with the drugs it's simply an act in futility. I have a chat with his caretakers before I leave the room. I tell them if they need anything don't hesitate to ask. I also make sure they understand if there's even the slightest downturn in his well being they are to send for me and the doctor immediately. They assure me they understand my instructions. I take one more look back at Cane before going to my own room. I needed to find Jack, so we can get to work pulling the weeds from our garden, so to speak. But first I need a shower and a change of clothes.

TEN

I make it to my flat without any further drama, take a quick shower and as if by magic, I find clean clothes out on the bed. I pick up my cell and my boots and almost make it to the living room when everything happened over the last several hours hits me. I sink heavily on the chaise near the door. Before now I didn't understand the purpose and position of the *stupid* thing. I'm trying hard not to think about what *could* have happened, but it doesn't take long before my thoughts are a jumbled mess. My phone starts to ring, and I welcome the opportunity to focus on something else as I answer it on speaker.

"Yeah?"

"Boss, its Brian. Team Five has called in an active shooter situation at the concert venue."

I run my hand through my hair and finish lacing my boots. "Shit, well of course there is. I'll meet you at my SUV directly. I'm coming down with nothing so grab what you think I'll need."

"On it," is all I hear before Brian disconnects.

My thoughts are spinning. *Team Five, was assigned a relatively simple job. Personal security for a musician. This is usually the type of job we can do in our sleep. Yet we now have an active shooter situation!*

I take the back stairs two at a time to reach the garage level. As I push through the door I see Brian standing next to my already running SUV. I put my hand out and he hands me an earpiece as well as my gear. The earpiece is already on and I can hear Jack barking out orders. I can also hear team members marking their positions and calling out who is headed to the garage.

Eric, with additional team members, enters the garage and begin to jump into the already rolling SUV's. Eric takes Cane's usual place behind me. I see Jack at the wheel of the Mercedes behind my SUV. My driver honks and the heavy doors roll up.

All the drivers lay rubber in the garage and I cringe. I know Donna is going to kill us when we get back for marking up her floor. We leave three vehicles deep, two armored SUV's and one armored Merc.

We pull out onto the street and our guys on the perimeter have stopped traffic. I'm a little surprised, but grateful, to find there are two bike officers waiting for us. Jack has clearly been a busy elf. We make quick work of the streets and the red lights thanks to our escort.

We arrive at the venue and as expected, there are police everywhere. We exit the vehicles in quick fashion; three guys remain behind with the Merc and the SUV's. The rest of us make our way into the lobby of the venue. We are brought up short by a young officer in a new overly pressed uniform.

Officer over-pressed raises his hand as we attempt to go under the crime scene tape. "You will need to go back the way you came."

I try to count to seven quickly, "I need to speak to whoever's in charge."

"Ma'am, you cannot be here. You need to go back the way you came and wait outside. People from the club need to vacate the area. In case you failed to notice this is a very serious situation. I'm sure if your services are still needed once this situation is cleared up, the music people know how to contact you."

At this point I'm about to lose my fucking mind. In my peripheral I can see Eric take a step back and on the other side Jack is smirking. I turn to my guys. "Gentlemen, I'm fairly sure this rookie called me a hooker. Did you guys hear the same thing or am I having a stroke?"

Both Jack and Eric are silent. I take out my phone and use speed dial to call the one cop I know is on scene. As it rings I put it on speaker. After a couple rings he picks up. "Hey good lookin', I'm a little busy, but I have a feeling you already knew that."

"Chief, you're on speaker and I would really like to assist you with your current problem. It's my team in there. *However*, there is a small hurdle in our way."

"Can this hurdle hear me?"

"Yes."

The Deputy Chief's voice comes over the phone. "Identify yourself?"

I hold the phone closer to the rookie's face. "I'm pretty sure he's talking to you."

"Officer Dearing, Metro P.D. Who am I speaking with?" The rookie replies.

Poor Jack is trying to keep it together and Eric bless him, is waiting for his marching orders.

"Officer this is Deputy Chief Garcia. I imagine you now realize what you've stepped in."

I pull the phone away from the officer because he's starting to lose the color in his face and I don't want him throwing up on my phone. "Chief, I think he grasps the situation. Would you be so kind as to tell me who I need to find out here in the lobby?"

"No worries, I'm on my way to you now."

"See you soon." I close the connection.

It takes the Chief less than twenty seconds to reach us. He kisses me on the cheek and shakes hands with Jack and Eric.

"I really appreciate you coming out to meet us." He hands me colored stripes of adhesive fabric. I take one and give the rest to Jack. He and Eric make sure everyone who needs one gets one. They rejoin us as the Chief gets on his radio to let the other officers on site know we'll be entering the building and we'll be wearing the color of the day to prevent another awkward encounter. I hug the large man and turn to wave at Officer Dearing as we enter the concert venue.

"I want to feel bad for the little fucker, but I know he's probably already wet himself," Jack says, as he can never walk away from any given situation without comment. We stand still waiting for our eyes to adjust to the darkness.

"Yeah, poor bastard has multiple ass chewings in his future," Eric says.

They're both let loose with the laughter as I shove them further into the room. *Really? Neither* one of you has *any comment* about the fact he insinuated I was a hooker?"

Jack answers without even looking at me. "Actually, I was thinking a hooker was better than a groupie."

I smack him on the back of the head as I walk past him. Eric keeps walking without a word, but I know he's smiling.

Inside the building Eric and I use the map we have to locate our client. Jack leads the rest of the team through the open fire door.

Eric leans in, "From the sound of it, the shooter has barricaded himself, as well as our client, in one of the dressing rooms."

I nod, "Well hell, let's get over there. I don't want our client hurt."

When we round the last corner where the dressing rooms are located, we are stopped by a large officer in full tactical gear. He's standing in front of a hastily hung bomb blanket. He looks me in the eyes and then down to the colored stripe on my shirt.

Before I can ask him anything, I hear Jack in my ear. He tells me he's learned at least one of our team is also down inside the room with our client. He goes on to say another one of our guys is being treated by EMT's inside the main theatre. I tell Eric to advise him we still have one man unaccounted for.

The big officer clears his throat and motions to the space behind him. "Ma'am. I think your other man is down in the hallway in front of the dressing room. My apologies, but we haven't received orders to try and get him out."

Eric and I push past the officer, Eric passes along this latest intel to Jack and the guys who are with him. Jack tells us our guy in the theatre doesn't look good and the EMT's are taking him to the closest E.R.

"Send someone with him," I tell Jack.

He tells me he already did and is now on his way to us.

Eric makes a clicking sound with his tongue and

our guy in the hallway turns to see where the sound came from. He holds up one finger and points to his hip. His action tells us he's been shot at least once. Somehow, he's managed to prop himself against the wall across from the dressing room. As I get ready to move down the hallway, Jack joins us.

"What's with muscle and fitness?" Jack asks, referring to the big Metro PD officer behind us.

I point down the hallway, to our man down, ignoring Jack's question. "He's been hit, and we need to know the extent of the damage."

Jack taps the boot of the officer and asks him to tell his commander we need more EMT's down here. The officer does as he's asked. I start to slide down the hallway on my knees and Eric follows. Jack is remaining at the entrance in case we need anything else from officer muscles. As I get closer I see its Kenny. He *has* looked better. Most of us call him Joker because of his wide evil grin. It is equal parts creepy and sexy as hell. I think it makes him look mischievous. Jack has always said it makes him look like, given the opportunity, he might eat the people he shoots.

I slide to his far side and whisper to him. "So, is there a reason you are sitting down on the job?"

He gives me his famous grin and nods at the door directly across from our position. "I wanted to make sure if he stuck his head out I was here to greet him." He grimaces as Eric begins to take stock of his injuries.

"Good news brother, you're not leaking from any place vital. Bad news is you *are* still leaking fluids you shouldn't be. Boss, we gotta' get him out of here."

Jack's voice comes over my earpiece, "The EMT's

are here." I look up and signal I heard him. I ask Eric if he can slide Kenny out on his own. He looks a bit insulted. I wink at him and rest my forehand on the side of Kenny's head for a second. "Okay, break time's over. Eric is going to get you to Jack and the EMT's will stop you from leaking."

Kenny grins at me again as Eric proceeds to grab the collar of his vest and begins to slide him down to Jack and the now waiting EMT's.

I refocus my attention because I need to find, first and foremost, if our client is safe. Also, I would like to get my men out of here preferably without any more holes in them. I slide across the floor and squat down next to the door. I take the baton out of my back pocket and use it to bang on the door.

When no one responds to my banging on the door, I yell. "Leo, you in there?"

Four bullets through the door is the only response I get to my question. I don't appreciate being shot at, but with the holes in the door I can now hear voices inside the room. I can't really make out what they're saying, but at least I know more than one person is alive.

I yell again. "Leo, I really need to know if you're okay!"

I hear some incoherent yelling, but I don't recognize the voice. I take this to mean it's the shooter who's doing most of the talking.

"Leo!" I yell again.

The shooter doesn't say anything this time, but I manage to hear two short whistles. This is Leo telling me he has been hit twice. I know he's alive and it makes me feel a little better.

I turn my focus to the shooter. "Ok, sir, you have two hostages. Exactly what is it you hope to accomplish?" I say near the door.

The shooter yells for silence and then he says is a high pitch voice, "I want him to stop fucking my girlfriend!"

I look at Jack, who has now joined me on the other side of the door. He is smacking himself in the head with his weapon.

"Okay, so you've shot at least three people we know of. You've also taken a guitar player and his wounded bodyguard hostage. Do you have proof Mr. Samuels has been having relations with your girlfriend?" I hope the question doesn't piss him off. I hear a lamp break and the guy starts cussing. However, I'm pretty sure he's talking to himself.

"Mr. Samuels are you alright?" I figure if he's talking to someone so should I. Our client hired us to keep him safe. The least I can do is make sure he's still alive.

Don't get me wrong Mr. Samuels has taken part in his fair share of affairs with many men's girlfriends. However, he's also a very careful man and he would never let any one of his indiscretions catch up to him like this. If he even had a sniff this could happen, he would have told me.

After a few beats I hear Mr. Samuels. "Alex, I'm fine, and for the record I'm *not* having relations with this man's girlfriend."

Jack can't help himself, "I love this guy."

I roll my eyes.

I hear a click in my earpiece and Miami tells me

he's in position. Miami is the skinniest man I have ever seen but he's one of the best shots we have. While we were chatting with the shooter and getting our men medical attention, Miami was carefully making his way over the ceiling. We now have eyes and our own active shooter in, or more accurately from above, the room. Miami's job is to take out the target if at any point he appears to be turning his weapon on our client or our injured man.

"Boss," Miami whispers, "Leo doesn't look good and I have the shot."

I don't even bother looking at Jack. He walks like a frog down the hallway to the large muscled guard to let him know we have another man inside the room and we are going to need another team of EMT's. Jack returns and takes his position across from the door. He's now standing and slightly to the side with his boot ready to take out the door. I stand up, ready to go in.

I key the mic button, "Green light, Miami, green light." I hear the spit of Miami's weapon as does Jack. It's our cue and Jack kicks the door in. We enter the room and find the shooter on the ground bleeding from the shoulder. I secure him while Jack checks the rest of the room. Mr. Samuels is sitting in a chair in the corner. Miami has dropped from the ceiling and is standing in front of him like a shield.

Jack nods at Miami and takes his place with Mr. Samuels. He tells Miami to send in the EMT's. Miami slides past me and a few seconds later the EMT's join us in the dressing room. At some point during the ordeal Leo removed his shirt and is using it to keep pressure on the bullet hole in his side. Both EMT's immediately begin to work on him.

I tap the EMT on the shoulder, "You might want to call another team for assistance," I point to the now zip-tied shooter. "Also make sure he goes to the same E.R. where they took our guy from the theatre. Keeping everyone in one place will make things easier. You need anything else?" I ask the closest EMT.

He looks up at me, "A gurney and your phone number."

I look down at him, "If he lives I'll consider it, however, if he dies you're going to need your own gurney." He winks at me and gets on his radio to call for more assistance.

Jack lets me know he's going to take Mr. Samuels out to the waiting Merc. He will escort him to a secure suite in one of our buildings.

Miami has been standing in the doorway keeping watch. As I walk past him he joins me and bumps my shoulder with his. "You know Cane would've shot the EMT in the face for asking for your number."

I tap the end of his nose with my finger as Miami laughs and blows a bubble with the gum he's been chomping on.

As the EMT's move Leo out on a gurney I tell them they need to follow our trucks out front, rather than go to the nearest hospital. They look a bit confused, but do exactly as I instructed them to do. I tell Miami to call our medical staff and let them know what's coming. The second set of EMT's are loading up the shooter so he can be sent to whatever E.R. is treating this mess. Metro P.D. can take care of him when they get time.

There will be no detailed reports about my team's involvement because, let's be honest, Metro P.D. doesn't want to do the paperwork and I don't blame them.

I let the Chief know what happened in the dressing room and I have a brief chat with the venue owner. I reassure the owner someone from our organization will be out directly to assess the damage and repairs will be started before close of business tomorrow. Both men are very appreciative we are going to take care of things. I go outside and get into my transport. I look at my driver and point out the window, "Home, James."

As he pulls out past the last of the cop cars into traffic he says, "Alex, you need to call Eric. He has an update for you."

I look at him, confused. "Didn't Eric tell *you*?"

"No, and he didn't sound good."

I grimace and take my phone out of my pocket to call Eric. It rings only once before he picks up. The other end of the phone is only silence, but I can hear him breathing. "Eric what's going on?"

"Patrick died on the operating table," is all he says, but he doesn't hang up.

"Eric, the shooter is in the E.R. Do you need me to meet you?" I ask knowing damn well what his answer will be.

"No," is all he says before the call disconnects.

I lean my head back and close my eyes. The ride back to the office is quiet. We arrive back at the garage and Jack's there waiting for me. We head straight for the stairs, taking them two at a time down to the medical floor.

I check with the head nurse and she let me know

Kenny is in surgery, but he's going to be fine. I finally stop moving, bend over and put my hands on my knees.

Jack reaches me and puts his hand on the back of my neck, "I can't reach Eric. What do you know I don't?"

I reach out with my hand and hold on to his leg. "Patrick died in surgery at the hospital. I let Eric know the shooter was in the E.R. I'm sure it's all over by now."

Jack gently tugs on my shirt and I stand up because I know I need to save these feelings for later. They'll do me no good at this point.

The head nurse lets us collect ourselves before she tells us what room they're going to put Kenny in. I'm sure it had more to do with getting us out of the middle of her workspace and less about keeping us informed. I can appreciate her logic. Jack and I wait for Kenny in his room.

We don't say anything. We just sit and wait. A long hour and a half later, he's wheeled into the room. He looks a bit pale, but the doctor reassures us he's going to be fine. Neither Jack nor I leave. It's another two hours before Kenny wakes up. Jack is the first to speak.

"Hey man, the doc says you're going to be fine. They didn't need to remove any bits of anything and all your parts still work."

Kenny flashes his Joker smile, albeit a bit weakly.

Jack asks him if he needs anything and he points to the water pitcher on the side table. Jack fills a glass and pulls a straw from the bedside table.

I'm watching the two of them, but I'm not really seeing them. My brain has gone completely manic. There's no way I can stay fixated on one thing. I'm pulled from my myriad of thoughts by a knock on the door. Jack motions for whoever it is to come in.

Eric sticks his head in, "Hey brother, it's good to see you awake."

Kenny gives him thumbs up.

Eric turns to me, "Boss, can I get a minute?"

I push out of the chair, stopping to mess up Kenny's hair. I can see the question on his face. "Jack is going to stay with you. I know he isn't much to look at, but he can be entertaining."

I leave the room and pull the door closed behind me. Eric turns without a word and I follow him to the freight elevator. We step in and he pushes the button for the detention level. We ride down in silence. The doors open, and he holds it until I step out. I stop since I have no idea where this is going. He looks at me or more accurately through me. He turns and starts to walk to the far corner, stopping to open the door leading to the burn room. Once we're both inside and the door is secure, he reaches into a pocket of his cargo pants. He pulls out an empty, fully compressed syringe wrapped in a towel. I take the towel and the syringe from him.

In a level, flat tone I say, "Tell me what happened." Eric fully understands this will be the only time he has to tell this story.

Eric looks me right in the eye and I can see parts of him shutting down. He takes a deep breath before he begins. "I told you Patrick died in surgery. You asked if I needed you to join me and I said I would take care of things. I hung up and used the stairs to go down to the E.R. Once there I found the area with the most chaos and swiped a used syringe from a tray. I walked around the E.R. until I found the shooter. The muscle officer from the venue was standing watch outside his room. He offered his condolences for Patrick and opened the door for me. I entered the room and the coward had the nerve to cry and apologize."

He takes another breath and continues. "I took a small towel from the side table and stuffed it in his mouth. I yanked out his IV and pulled the plunger back on the syringe. I slid the needle into the same hole the IV was in and pushed the plunger all the way down. I held the towel in his mouth until his eyes started to bulge. I pulled the towel from his mouth and unplugged the machines from the wall. I also used the towel to shove the IV back in his arm. I put the syringe in the towel and put them both in my pocket. He was dead before I left the room. I knocked on the door and the muscle officer again opened it for me."

"I then proceeded down to the morgue to claim Patrick's body. I told them we would take care of the autopsy and notifying his family. I *had* to bring him back. I couldn't leave him there alone. When I pulled into the garage Donna stopped me and told me to come and see you. She told me she would take care of him until I came back."

He takes final deep breath and to be honest I couldn't remember if I'd taken a breath the entire time he was talking.

I open the door to the small incinerator and make sure he's watching. I toss in the towel, the syringe and shut the door. "Patrick would have done the same for you. Now go and sit with your brother." I push the door open and wait for him to follow me out. He walks out and past me without another word.

ELEVEN

I collect my thoughts before stopping by the medical floor. I need to make sure the staff has everything they need to take care of Kenny and Leo. One of my stray thoughts is to send Jack to talk to the large Metro cop. We can always use a good man, if he ever decides to go private.

I find Jack leaning against the wall outside Kenny's room. He assures me everything is being taken care of and Kenny is resting. Before I can leave, he asks, "Is Eric watching over Patrick?"

I answer as I turn to leave. "Where else would he be?" I push through the door to the stairs, taking them slowly, making sure to step on each one with both feet. About halfway up, I stop and give in letting the pain take over. The loss of one of us is like losing a limb. I don't cry because I never know who I'll have to talk to at any given moment. When I cry it disturbs the men and to me it can be a sign of weakness. Any personal sadness will need to wait until I'm safely locked in my flat, alone. I compose myself, square my shoulders and continue my trek up the stairs.

I stop at the door to Cane's floor. I know I should stop and see how he's doing. But, the internal battle of wills within myself is telling me I need some alone time. I lean my head against the door because I can hear Veronica's voice in my head. She's telling me *'It 'ain't about me' and to go do your damn job and check on*

Cane'. I push open the stairwell door heading to Cane's room and make a mental note to call Veronica and cuss her out for being my *conscience*.

I wave at the two men standing watch outside his door. I knock and hear a voice on the other side telling me to come in. As I enter, I find Cane putting his TV remote through its paces, not to mention he's starting to look a bit stir crazy. I walk over to stand next to him as the door closes behind me.

I cross my arms over my chest, "So you look like you might be ready to jump out of your window," I say with a raised eyebrow.

He looks at me with his frustration written all over his face. "I tried to leave this damn room but the gargoyles at the door wouldn't let me out. They said since you and the old man were out on an emergency, there was no one they could call to get clearance." He throws the remote across the room and turns to face me. "Not to mention, neither one of them turned their radios down. I heard the updates as they came in over the open channel."

I nod to show him I'm listening. When I speak, I stand up a bit taller to show him I'm not impressed with his outburst. I bite my cheek to keep from saying the wrong thing because I know he's frustrated. So, in a calm, but very authoritative voice, I begin. "I'm going to let the remote throwing go because I'm sure you're frustrated with your personal situation. I'm also going to overlook you venting your anger at me. As I would assume, had Jack been the first one to come and check on you, he would have been subjected to the same. However, know your tantrum is minuscule in the big picture. We have two men recovering from surgery and we have a man dead downstairs. His friend of over fifteen years is sitting next to an open body drawer probably drunk and talking to him about the good times. So, you're gonna' have to forgive me if I don't give a *fuck* about your very small issue of being left out or being overly cared for and restricted to your fucking room."

Cane doesn't say a word. I look at him for a good sixty seconds before I walk to the private door to enter my flat. Before I shut the door, I look back at him. "We're back and I've informed your guards you can roam around all you like." Without another word I slam the door and take the stairs to my private quarters.

Once in my flat, I kick off my shoes and socks. I unbutton my jeans, throw my bra on the floor and turn on the TV. Wrapping myself in my bed covers I call it a night.

I wake up to the smell of what I can only describe as a dead body. Don't get me wrong, it's not a smell I encounter often, but in this case, I'm pretty sure it's what I'm smelling. I roll out of bed with various blankets still wrapped around me. I put my glasses on and make my way to the living room. I can see the back of Jack's head as he sits on the couch watching TV.

I flick him behind the ear and pinch my nose as I get a whiff of his tea. "Why did you steep someone's dead ass to make your swill and more importantly what the fuck are you doing drinking it in my living room?"

"Well, I thought you might be dead, so if I found it to be the case, I wanted to be the first one to claim your ass because, to be honest, I think it would make good tea."

I reach for one of the decorative pillows and chuck it at his head and miss by inches.

He picks it up off the floor and puts the pillow behind his head as he leans back. "Thanks, my neck was starting to hurt. I have to tilt it all the way back to look at this monstrosity of a TV."

I pull the blankets tight around me, walk around to where Jack is and flop onto the couch. I quickly realize I spent too much time in bed; my lower back and my bladder are very angry. I get up carefully and walk back to my bedroom.

"Jack, be useful and buzz for Jacob," I yell at him as I go into the bathroom.

"You know he's a Jedi, right? "Jack says. "*Think* his name and he'll walk through a damn wall."

I shake my head as I shut the door.

I take my time in the bathroom, because as far as I'm concerned there can be no emergencies today. When I finish and head into my changing room, I see Jacob has clearly been there. Last night's clothes are gone, and several choices have been laid out for me. To keep with my theme of no emergencies I choose some very loose and ragged jeans along with my favorite rugby team singlet. I pick out some socks and go back out to the main room to put them on. Jack has turned the TV off and is sitting on a bar stool in the kitchen area reading something.

I feel much more like a human now I've showered and dressed. I enter the kitchen leaning on the counter to pull on my socks. I open the fridge and choose a very large bottle of water, opening it to take a long drink. I nudge Jack's reading material and when he looks up. I take the opportunity to poke myself in the gut and burp disgustingly loud. Jack shakes his head and looks at me like I'm completely unstable.

He pushes a piece of paper across the counter. "This is the report for the mountain man—"

I slap my hand down on the paper stopping him mid-sentence. "I don't care what the damn report says."

Jack raises his eyebrow at me. I relent and ask him to give me the highlights. He says that we will be keeping the mountain man on site as our guest. At least until the fact checking people can sift through everything that was learned in the interrogation. Once it's all sorted then we will dispose of him in a manner befitting his crimes.

I glance at the paper and then push it away. "Works for me. Now, nothing else today, Jack. I want to eat something and maybe go to the range. That's it. No reports, no drama and no blood. Have you seen Eric this morning?"

Jack purses his lips and considers what I'm saying. He shrugs his shoulders and throws the report on the floor. "Yeah, I found him asleep last night next to the body cooler. I put a blanket over him and left him there. I stopped down there before coming up here and he was still asleep in the same place. I doubt he moved at all last night."

I push the button on the phone to get Jacob.

"Yes, Miss?"

"Jacob, please check on Cane and make sure Eric gets to his flat."

He responds, "Of course, Miss."

"You aren't going to check on Cane yourself?" Jack asks. He seemed genuinely surprised.

"No, he made a bit of scene when I saw him last

night. Of course, I then made a bigger bit of a scene. I think it would be best if there was some space between us today."

Jack seems like he's searching for some particular words but eventually gives up and says, "So what you're telling me is he experienced his first '*Come to Jesus*' meeting."

I smile at him and nod. I open the fridge and take out one of the premixed shakes Jacob has prepared for me. I place it on the blender for a few pulses to mix things up. I throw the lid in the sink and drink it as quick as possible; I know they're healthy, but they're best consumed quickly with your nose pinched so you can't smell them. I rinse out the cup and leave it in the sink for Jacob. I retrieve my heavy-duty boots from the closet and take a seat on the sofa to put them on.

Jack is watching me go through the motions. "Since you're putting those on, I'm assuming you're going down to the range."

I finish lacing my boots and stand. "Yes, old man. I'm going to go and shoot paper people until I can't lift my arms above my head."

I watch him take a deep breath and I know something grown up is about to come out of his face. I shove my hands in my pockets and wait.

His voice is serious. "We need to make arrangements for Patrick."

I drop my chin to my chest and close my eyes. After a heartbeat I look up at him. "Once Eric is ready to talk about what he wants to do, come get me or send someone for me. He should be the one to make the decisions. I think the only thing we need to address is the chatter and speculation going around the building. Keeping the discussions to a minimum will make this easier on all of us."

Jack scratches his two-day old beard. "You're right about Eric and I'll take care of the chatter. On your way down to the range stop by and see Kenny."

I pick my I-Pod and earphones off the table. "I'll stop and see Joker. Don't forget to take your dead-people-tea with you when you leave." I leave and take the back stairs down to the medical level. Despite everything, I know seeing Kenny's crazy smile will make things a little better.

The medical level is very quiet. I knock on the sliding door to Kenny's room since the curtain is closed. It isn't too long before the doc pulls back the curtain and opens the door. Given his state of undress I can only assume the doc was checking on the bullet wound. The doc lets me know he's healing as he should be. I shake his hand as he tells Kenny he'll be back later. The doc slides the door shut and Kenny turns the TV off as I shove my hands into my pockets. Kenny, at a little less than six feet and very fit at one hundred and eighty pounds, is not vain but he is also not shy.

I look at his naked form, "You're gonna' catch a cold laying there all exposed."

He flashes me one of his damn grins. "I have to let my wound get fresh air. I can't miss any work because of an infection. I barely got time off for this bullet wound."

I sit down in the chair because in truth his abs and hip indents are more than a bit distracting. "With all the activity last night, we will be standing down for a few days. Jack and I will be around if you need anything. We haven't had a chance to talk to Eric yet. Once arrangements have been made, I'll get with the doc to make sure we can get you there."

Kenny's face goes serious and he seems to be a bit lost. "Boss, what are you talking about? Make arrangements for what?"

I hang my head. *Damn!* "Has Jack not been down to see you today?"

"No, you're the only person I've seen other than the docs since late yesterday." He tries to lean a little closer to me. He gets a sharp pain for his troubles if his grimace is any indication.

I pinch the bridge of my nose and make a mental note to shoot Jack in the foot. Patrick, Eric and Kenny were three of a kind. He will feel this almost as much as Eric. I take a deep breath, "Patrick didn't make it out of surgery yesterday. I was sure Jack would have told you last night."

Kenny has a look of disbelief. "Where is Patrick? Is Eric with him?"

"Eric brought Patrick back here. He spent last night with him downstairs. Jack said he was still with him this morning. I sent Jacob to make sure Eric makes it to his flat."

Kenny seems to be satisfied with my answer. He puts his free arm over his eyes and leans back on the pillows. I take this as my cue to leave. As I stand Kenny asks, "The shooter?"

I give him the short answer. "I imagine his autopsy is scheduled for some time today."

Kenny moves his arm down, so he can see me. "Thank you."

I lean down and whisper against his ear. "There is no mercy for someone who takes out one of ours."

He covers his eyes again and I see the corners of his mouth turn up slightly. I turn the light off before I leave the room without another word.

I check in with Kenny's doctor before I go back upstairs and find him sitting at his desk almost bookended by files.

"You know, doc, the reason we went paperless was, so you wouldn't die from a fatal papercut."

He looks up with tired eyes but a smile on his face. "Hey Alex, I was reading the paperwork from the surgeon at the E.R."

I look at him, a bit confused. I know I didn't ask for the information to be sent over. I sit down in one of the large arm chairs in front of his desk.

Doc continues, "I called him when we got word about Patrick. I wanted to know, or maybe more precisely, I *needed to know*, if we could have saved him."

"And…" I'm both hopeful and terrified about the decision I made about Patrick's care.

"Honestly, it's shit either way. If you had brought him here he would have died. The damage done was so extensive there was no way to save him. From what I have read, in my honest opinion, the E.R. doctor did more than he should have. He used some extreme measures to try and save our boy. I can't tell you if he suffered or not. Our guys are stronger and more stubborn than any ten-people put together have a right to be."

I grin at the last part. "Yeah, our guys are something else." A bit of annoyance seeps into my brain. I'm starting to think perhaps I need to *make nice with Cane*. Of course, there's another part of my brain telling the feeling part to *shut the hell up*.

The doc starts to speak again, thankfully. "I think perhaps we should reach out to the surgeon. He might be ready for a jump to the private sector."

"I think it's an excellent idea. I'll let you take care of contacting him since I don't speak *doctor*. Last thing, I wanted to ask you, how soon will Kenny be able to attend a service for Patrick?"

He uses his computer to get the most recent information on Kenny's condition. "He could be there in a wheelchair day after tomorrow. If it's any sooner, we'll have to wheel him down in his bed."

I stand and reach out my hand to the doc. "Thanks, I'm sure we can wait a couple days. I think a little time will be good for all of us."

The doctor doesn't take my hand. Instead he walks around his desk and steps in to give me a hug. I hug him back because we both seem to need the physical contact. I smile and leave his office without another word.

I take the elevator to my office in search of Jacob. When I don't find him there cleaning, I push the call button and wait. Jacob arrives about two minutes later. I look up from my phone screen to find him standing statue still in front of my desk.

"You know, Jack might be right about getting you a bell."

He doesn't say anything, nor does he smile. It bothers me more than little. "Jacob what's going on?"

"Miss, I think you should check on Mr. Eric yourself. He doesn't want anyone to bother him. He's very combative and has, it appears, been drinking in excess."

"Jacob, he's mourning the loss of his brother. Maybe not biological, but they had been by each other's side, one way or another, since they were ten. I don't blame him for being angry or drunk."

"Miss, I agree with you on both points. However, right now I believe Eric's intent is not to mourn Mr. Patrick, but to join him. We can't allow him to take this any further than he already has."

I blow out a deep breath and put my hands up relenting. *Fuck!* I don't want to send anyone else into his flat to get him. I know the other guys wouldn't want to take him on in his current state, so I make a command decision. "Jacob, please ask the twins to go in and ferret him out. Have them take him and his alcohol to one of the large cells downstairs. Have them make sure the padding is up; I don't want him to hurt himself trying to get out. Then please send a sanitation crew into his flat to clean it. How's that for a plan?"

"Most satisfactory," he says with a raised eyebrow.

"Good. Lastly, please send a message out to everyone the memorial for Patrick will be held the day after tomorrow. We will be shutting down the offices for the day. If the local people do not wish to come for the memorial, tell them to take the day off. Make sure we have enough accommodations for any of our people coming in from out of state or out of the country."

He doesn't leave right away. "Is there something else, Jacob?"

"Yes, Miss. Should I leave Mr. Patrick's flat the way it is?"

"Crap! I hadn't given it any thought. But, yeah, leave it." I rub my eyes and feel the grit. "For now, lock it up. When Eric is feeling better, if he can't clean it out, then Jack and I will take care of it."

"Yes, Miss." He turns and leaves the room as quietly as he entered.

My cell phone rings. I see Jack on the caller I.D. "What?"

"What do you mean, *what*? Where the hell are you?" He sounds annoyed.

"I'm in my office. Why are you so agitated?"

"Well I'm where you're supposed to be."

"Get to the point Jack before I get bored and hang up on your crazy ass."

"I'm down at the range; you said you were coming here after you stopped in to see Kenny. You aren't here, and they say you never came down."

I bang my phone on the desk. "I got distracted after I went down to see Kenny and I had to tell him about the death of his friend. I thought *you'd* done it already. I wasn't prepared for *this little chore* and I forgot all about going down to the damn range."

"Fuck, Alex, sorry," he says apologetically. "Don't disappear, I'm on my way."

I hang up. *What the fuck?* As I recline in my chair I consider going to somewhere else in the building to piss him off. It doesn't take me long to realize it'd be a waste of effort as he'd only hunt me down. I close my eyes, take deep breaths and wait.

Five or so minutes later I hear his rude pounding on my office door. I take a deep breath before I push the button to unlock the door and let him in. He doesn't say a word until he sits down in his ratty chair in front of my desk.

"I'm really sorry I forgot to tell you I hadn't had a chance to speak to Kenny about Patrick." He looks very uncomfortable.

"I accept your apology. But you should have seen him, Jack. If I had a heart, it would have broken. We both know how he feels, but it sucks to watch our tough guys get this type of news." I cross my arms in front of me on my desk and put my head down.

Jack waits patiently but finally asks, "Before I forget; I went to check on Eric and there was a sanitation team in his flat. What happened, or do I not want to know?"

I tilt my head, so I can see him. "I sent Jacob to check on Cane and Eric. He told me Eric was very drunk, unhealthily so. Also, Eric was extremely combative. Now, I know this is to be expected, but I'm not going to have him die because of an accident. I told Jacob to send the twins to fetch him from his room. They were also told to pad one of the larger cells downstairs and put him in it. He has his liquor, his grief and his anger. We have him in a safe place where we can watch him. Of course, now when I think about it, I forgot to ask Jacob about Cane. At this rate I wouldn't be surprised if he left."

I push myself up out of my chair. "Also, Jacob asked about Patrick's flat. I told him to seal it off and if Eric couldn't clean it out you I would take care of it later."

From the look on Jack's face, I realize he's starting to regret tracking me down.

"I think once Eric is finished being drunk, he'll want to take care of Patrick's stuff. Hell," Jack shrugs, "he may move into the flat to make sure it stays in the family. I'm gonna' go down and check on him." He stands up and we walk to the doors together. We squeeze together as we go through the door and I take the time to kick him in the ass as we part ways.

I decided if I'm going to check on Cane, I need to do it like an adult and use the front door. Before I knock I listen at the door. I'm almost sure I hear the TV. I swallow some pride and firmly pound on the door. After a short wait I almost turn to walk away when I hear the lock tumble. Cane opens the door and I must admit I almost need to check to make sure my mouth is closed.

He's breathing fast, standing there in only a pair of training shorts. Clearly, he's been working out. He doesn't say anything, simply steps back and opens the door wider as he motions me to enter. Part of my brain is telling me to get the hell out of there. Of course, the other part is trying to convince me he's another shirtless guy and just an everyday occurrence in the building. I step inside and he closes the door behind me.

He uses the back of his hand to wipe sweat from his brow. "I was doing some doctor approved exercises to keep from getting too soft."

I put my hands in my pockets mostly because it seems like the safest plan. "I didn't mean to interrupt your workout. I wanted to apologize for being a major bitch the last time we talked. I was mad and frustrated I couldn't change the outcome of what had happened to our team, so it was a bit unfair."

He listens, nods and takes a seat on the weight bench in the middle of the room. Cane picks up a large kettlebell in his left hand, hoists it over his head and starts to press it from the base of his neck straight up to the ceiling. Kenny was distracting enough with his hip indents and sinewy muscles all over. But Cane is just as bad. He's built more like a big block engine, large, well defined arms and an eight pack which makes me want to take up drinking.

I'm brought back from my thoughts by his voice. "Boss, you still with me?"

I blink and clear my throat. "Yeah, I was over thinking something. Sorry, what did you say?"

"I said we're good. I should've used my brain before I opened my mouth." He lets the kettlebell drop the last inch to the ground with a thud.

"So, I take it Jacob filled you in on the particulars of last night?" I manage to get an entire sentence out before having to clear my throat once again.

He picks up the kettle bell and starts to do some crazy bicep exercise before answering me. "Yeah, he told me about what happened. I liked Patrick; he was a good man. I know Eric and Kenny were really close to him. How are they doing? Are they handling the situation?" He takes a deep breath and the kettle bell thuds to the ground again.

Things are really starting to get a bit bulgy and sweaty and I try to keep focused on what I want to say. "You're right, both Kenny and Eric pretty much grew up with Patrick. They're taking it hard. Kenny is healing, but Eric is trying to drink his pain away. We've had him moved to a padded cell, so we can monitor him. We've planned the service for day after tomorrow. Kenny will be able to attend in a wheelchair. I'm hoping Jack can get Eric dried out by then. If not, then we'll wait."

He wipes the sweat from his face with a crumpled-up shirt before starting again with the blasted kettle bell.

"Is it safe to say the person responsible for all this is no longer a problem?"

I only nod in answer.

I notice something on the ground, but it takes me a minute to process what it is. I take my hands out my pockets and squat down, so I can get a closer look.

Cane abruptly stops and puts the weight down.

I look at him. "You're bleeding from somewhere. Stand up."

He does as I ask. He doesn't have a lot of clothing on. Not to mention the damn training shorts only cover so much. I stand up and walk around to his back. I notice a small trail of blood going down his spine. When I look closer I can see some of the sutures high on his neck have popped. I keep inspecting his person and I can see another trail a bit larger going down the inside of his leg. I grin because I know there's a joke in this someplace.

"Well congratulations Hercules, you managed to pop some of the sutures on your neck. It also appears you have entered puberty." I say the last part while pointing as his leg.

He puts his hand to the back of his neck and pulls it back to see the blood. Shaking his head, he turns his leg out and sees the significant amount of blood now running down his leg. "Well fuck!" He sits back down on the bench.

I locate his phone on the counter and push the call button for the medical floor. "Yes, Mr. Cane can we help you?" A pleasant male voice comes over the speaker.

"Hey, it's Alex, I'm here with Cane. He appears to have popped some of his neck and groin sutures. Please let the doctor know I'd like him to come up and take care of it. I'll wait here for him as it'd be a tragedy for him to bleed out." The voice on the phone tells me he'll send the doctor up directly. I thank him and hang up.

Cane looks up at me. "So. are you going to help me apply pressure to my wounds, so I don't bleed out?"

"Not happening. Besides I called the doctor. He'll be here shortly to take care of it." I put my hands back in my pockets to stifle any desire to help. It doesn't take long before I hear a knock on the door and the doctor enters the room. It's much easier with another person in the room with Cane and me.

It takes a moment for the doc to find the origin of the blood. He tells me it's not bad, he then instructs Cane to take a shower and come back so he can close the wounds.

"Did he open my handy work alone or did you assist him?" The doctor snickers at his own attempt at humor.

I push his shoulder, "Very funny, doc. You know damn well I don't go on any of the in-house rides."

He laughs as he finishes laying out all the items he'll need to put Cane back together. "I know. I just thought it would be easier than traipsing out to your island for a ride."

I can't help but laugh with him. "I accept your logic, but the ride on the island is death defying and other rides are more of the guided-pony variety."

My comment gets a bout of laughter which leads to coughing. After he catches his breath, the doctor says, "Point taken, Alex."

"What's so funny?" Cane asks, emerging from his

bedroom with what can best be described as a hand towel wrapped around his waist.

The doc sees I have become a bit distracted by Cane's lack of attire. "Nothing, I was telling Alex about a case I had in medical school."

"Oh, okay. Where do you want me doc?" Cane asks while gripping his tiny towel at his narrow waist.

"Well," I say, "this all looks very man-bits-only, so I'm going to go and check on Eric. Doc, have you been down to see him?"

"Yes, I was down there about thirty minutes ago. Jack was using the power washer on him and his current accommodations."

I nod and turn to leave.

Cane's voice stops me. "Boss, could you ask Donna to order some larger towels?"

I turn to answer him and he's still holding the small towel over his man parts. I shrug, "Looks to me like the towels are plenty big enough."

Before the door closes, I hear the doctor tell Cane he's trying to play in the 'no-limit-room' and he still needs to master the 'five-dollar' tables.

TWELVE

I get down to the detention level and ask the man at the desk where I can find Jack. He tells me he's taken Eric to get cleaned up. I walk back to the cavernous shower area. From a distance I can hear water, glass breaking and a lot of cussing. I turn the corner and find Jack hosing Eric down. It's clear, from the smell, Eric has clearly gotten sick on himself at least once but probably multiple times. At this point I'm not entirely sure Jack is trying to clean him off. It looks more like he's trying to sober him up by nearly drowning the poor guy.

I yell so Jack can hear me over the water. "Is this a new waterboarding technique?"

Jack hears me and turns, "Hey, he smelled like he was dead. I dragged him in to check and he wouldn't let go of the stupid bottle. The result is... Well... This."

"Did the bottle break when it unstuck from his hands or when he tried to throw it at you?" I ask with my hands on my hips in frustration at what a mess this is.

I see Eric trying to prop himself up on the floor and decide this has gone on long enough. "Jack, turn the fucking water *off.*"

He does, but not before spraying Eric once more in the chest.

I take a deep breath because otherwise I may turn the water on Jack. I wade into the shower and squat near Eric. "Do you have something to say?"

Eric replies in a very scratchy voice, "I said, I was aiming for his head."

I look up at Jack. "I think he's had enough water. His desire to kill you appears to be a well warranted and very lucid thought." I grabbed hold of Eric's arm. "Let's stand you up." I hook one of my arms under his shoulder and help him stand. He's soaked to the bone. His clothes are going to be burned so I reach into my back pocket for my knife.

Jack comes over without a word and helps Eric keep his balance.

I use the blade to slice up the spine of Eric's shirt.

Jack peels it off him by pulling on the sleeves, tossing it aside as he goes to get a towel from a nearby cart. He throws the towel over his shoulder and comes back to us letting Eric rest his hands on Jack's forearms for support.

I squat down and use the blade to make quick work of the outside seam of both legs of his jeans. I reach up and peel off one side. The jeans quickly form a pile at his bare feet. I've heard jokes about Eric being a commando guy. With the removal of his jeans, I can now see it's no joke.

I look over at Jack. "I hate to say it Eric, but I think now with your clothes off, Jack should probably spray you again."

Eric manages to express his disagreement. "I think I can manage a proper shower if I can get out of this broken glass," He gets the sentence out before having to catch his breath.

I nod at Jack before pulling out my phone to call Jacob. "It's me. Please send a couple of cleaning people to the showers on the detention level. Also make sure they bring in at least three long pieces of workout floor material, there's some broken glass to contend with. Thank you." When I turn back around part of me is sad Eric is covered but the better part of me is glad to see he is trying to pull himself out of his self-destructive behavior.

It takes less than ten minutes for the cleaning staff to appear. I take the pieces of flooring I asked for and make a walkway. This will give Eric safe passage to the hallway and the private showers in the workout area.

"Eric, walk on the rubber parts and you'll be fine. Go back and take a shower. Jack will wait for you to make sure you don't fall asleep or fall down." Eric starts to object, and I give him a raised eyebrow. "The alternative is, Jack gets in the shower with you and helps you clean your man bits."

Eric puts up his hands as best he can in surrender and Jack follows him as he gingerly walks over the flooring.

I ask the cleaning people to make sure the clothes are burned. I also tell them about the broken bottle. Sadly, this is not our first rodeo and I know, in our line of work, it won't be our last. These men are tough but they're close and when one doesn't make it, they all die a little with him.

I've checked on everyone and decide it's probably the best time to go down to the range. I need to get some rounds in before something else shitty happens.

I spend the rest of the day at the range. Like the men who work for us, I must maintain a certain proficiency with every weapon I might be handed. After cleaning off my hands for the fourth time I decide I've had enough. My hands are cramping and raising my arms to scratch my nose is becoming extremely difficult and a little painful. It takes me a minute to get the door open to the back stairs. When your arms reach this level of exhaustion, you really need to concentrate to get them to do normal everyday things.

I take the stairs slowly to keep my balance. This also serves the purpose of forcing me to concentrate on the things I haven't been thinking about for the last several hours. When I reach my floor, I lean against the push bar with my hip. I stop short when I hear voices.

I take a deep breath, push the door open the rest of the way and enter the room. "Did I miss a meeting?" I ask the room.

"No, Eric and I came to see you and lost track of time waiting for your crazy ass," is Jack's answer.

I can see a shirtless Eric sitting on the far end of my couch. "Eric, please tell me you have pants on."

He gives me a weak smile. "Yes, boss, I have pants on."

"Well if you both will excuse me, I need a shower." I start to walk towards my room.

"Alex, Eric wanted to talk to us about…Well, everything." Jack gets it all out on a long exhale.

"Eric, I need a shower, and if you don't need to talk right this minute, it can wait until I'm done."

"Well, I don't know how much talking we would get done right this minute. Honestly, boss you smell like the undercarriage of your forty-five caliber. You know, if it had an undercarriage."

I laugh, "If I could lift my arms I'd smack you."

"I *could* go get Cane if you need some help with your shower. Doc said you had your hands shoved so far into your pockets your fingers were in your socks." Eric says all this with a smile on his face.

Jack is laughing so hard he almost falls off the couch onto the floor.

I shake my head and roll my eyes at Eric and he is quick with a retort, "Yes or no?"

I keep shaking my head all the way into my bathroom.

The multiple shower heads and heaps of steamy water help to unlock my sore arms. I scrub everything twice before getting out. I didn't shut the door to my room so when I emerge from the bathroom, I find Jack sitting in my reading chair.

"Where's Eric?"

"He's out there watching TV. I wanted to check in with you about Cane."

I give him what I'm sure is a confused look. "What *about* him?"

"Alex, you can't take that ride." He says as if this is something I need to be told.

I walk into my dressing room without saying a word. I'm not angry, I'm just annoyed. I pull on some sitting-on-my ass clothes and walk out to face Jack who is now standing with his arms crossed over his chest.

"Don't get all Mr. Boss man with me. I have *never* taken up with any of the men who work for us. Also, in case you have forgotten, I get everything I need on the island. So, if you'll excuse me, I need to go see what Eric wants to talk about." As I walk past him he puts his arm out. I stop and take a deep breath, so I don't hit him, and look him in the eyes.

Jack adopts a serious demeanor. "I know you have your rules *and* you have your island. I also know Cane is not just another one of the men. There's something there and even if it never comes to fruition, it can still get complicated. So, to stack something else on top of *the* steaming pile of shit, I'm more worried about when Cane gets some entertainment of his own. Is it going to be an issue?"

I think about what he says because I know this has the potential to be a mess if my head is in the wrong space. "We both know I'll have an issue with it. *Maybe*. However, I will make every effort to find other outlets for my frustration."

Jack's head falls forward as he puts his arm down. "Why doesn't that make me feel any better?"

I ignore him, push past him and join Eric on the couch. It takes him a minute to realize he's no longer alone. Jack flops down on the other side of him and starts the conversation ball rolling.

"Okay, Eric. Alex and I are here to help you, but we will not force any decisions on you. We have a service planned, but it will not happen until you feel you are ready. You're the closest thing Patrick had to family, so we'll be taking our cues from you. If you want to sit here and drool on yourself until it's time for the service, we can take care of things."

Eric takes a deep breath and I can see the focus come back into his eyes. He looks down at himself and then over at me. "Where the hell is my shirt?"

I laugh so hard I start to cough. "Son, you were fucking shirtless when I *got* here."

"Oh, hell, sorry boss, I'll go get a shirt and come back."

I put my arm out to keep him in his seat. "Good grief you don't need a shirt unless Jack is turned on. I mean at his age his sexuality is more fluid."

Jack spits his beer all over himself. "Woman," Jack snaps. "The only thing fluid about me is my blood alcohol level." He sits up and pulls his shirt off.

"Oh, look Eric; at least we know the salt and pepper look is an all over thing not only in his beard," I say as I jump towards Eric to get out of range of Jack's swinging boot.

Eric catches me so we both don't hit the floor or much worse the glass coffee table. He's kind enough to slide me over his lap. He puts himself between me and Jack. I put my thumbs to my temples and wave my fingers while making a raspberry sound at Jack.

"When are you going to grow up?" Jack says, throwing a pillow at me.

"It's amazing you two ever make it down to the garage in one piece." Eric tells us both in a very parental voice.

Without a second thought Jack reaches over and pinches Eric's nipple. Eric makes a sort of squeaking sound. I flop right down on the floor square on my ass in a full belly laugh. Eric leans over me, "When you're done Chuckles, we really need to talk about the grown-up stuff."

I put my hands up in surrender and he's kind

enough to help me up. I look over at Jack who has gone to get another beer from the fridge. I admit I see what Veronica sees. Old men like Jack are not my thing, but I can see why she likes twisting him into a pretzel.

I know everything we need to talk about is sad, but I'm glad we can still make each other laugh despite what's going on. I start the dialogue this time. "Okay, first thing is, what would you like to do with Patrick's flat? We can clean it out and eventually move someone in or you can take it."

Eric stares at the floor for a bit and looks at me before turning his eyes back to the floor.

I nudge his knee with mine. "Go ahead and say what you're thinking. It's only us here."

Eric takes a breath, "Truly?" I'd like to knock down the wall and make one big flat. I know it sounds selfish to want to keep both spaces. It's just at one time or another we shared both. Between my insomnia and his night terrors it was a rare night we didn't keep watch over each other."

I look over and Jack winks at me. "I don't think it's too much to ask at all. I'll let Jacob know and you two can work out the details."

Eric leans back on the couch and lays his head all the way back, so he is looking up at the ceiling. "So, what's next?"

"Well, if you have talked to the doc, then you know Kenny will be mobile, albeit in a wheelchair the day after tomorrow. Unless you have a specific date in mind, I think we should have the service then, but it's your decision. As you are the one who would know best as to what Patrick would want."

Eric takes a deep breath. "Patrick would want us to wait for Kenny. The day after tomorrow is as a good a day as any." He quickly moves on to the next subject on his own. "He always said he wanted his marker to look like this." Eric pulls a five by five-inch tile from his back pocket. "He called it blood marble." Eric turned the piece in his hand. "It looks a bit like red lightening. It's very pretty, very sad and eerie all at the same time."

I take the tile from his hand and give it to Jack. "Get this to your guy. I want this by day after tomorrow. It needs to be seven by seven-foot square and one and a quarter inches thick. I want it hung and ready for after the service."

Jack takes the tile from me and pulls his phone out to start making phone calls.

Eric lifts his head. "You know the size of the marker you described would make Patrick feel weird."

Now it's my turn to look down at the floor. "Exactly why he'll get such a large one. What about food? Do you want to have Donna and her elves make his favorites?"

Eric thinks for a second and smiles to himself. "Yea, yea, I think it would be nice. Patrick always said he liked the after part of a job. When the teams who did the hard work got together watched a match or some movies and ate together as a family."

I nod at him. "I'll let Donna know about the food. We'll set it up in the banquet room. You can choose what we watch. I will make sure Kevin has our entire library available as well as anything Patrick watched multiple times on his DVR. Well, you know, not the *porn*, but the other stuff."

Eric laughs out loud, and I can see it goes all the way to his eyes. It's good to hear and see. I glance at Jack who I can tell is thinking the same thing. We both knew he would come out on the other side of this. It's nice to know it will be sooner rather than later. I ask Eric if there's anything else.

He stands and stretches. "If we could get the guys to dress up, I think it would have made Patrick laugh. Also, Alex, if you can get me an appointment with your tattoo guy, I would appreciate it."

I grin like a fool and clap. "I do love me a fancy suit day. You just let me know when you want to see Watts and I'll call him. I'll have him come to us, it's easier."

Eric grins and starts for the door. He turns with a strange look on his face. "Alex, my apartment is kind of a mess if I remember correctly. Would you mind if I crash on your couch?"

"Well I suppose since you were nice enough to show up without a shirt I can let you use the couch." I throw a pillow at him before getting up to get him some blankets.

As I come back into the room, Jack gets off the phone. "My guy will be here by tomorrow night. He says he will have it ready by first light. What's with the blanket? Is Eric going to stay here?"

"Yeah, I'm not sure if the cleaning crew is finished with his space and even if they are, it should probably be aired out as well as refurnished. We might want to look into finding him an alternate space since construction will need to get started sooner rather than later."

Jack nods and wishes us both good night before leaving us alone.

I watch Eric making up his temporary bed. "You can sleep there as long as you like. Let Jacob know when you want to get into your temporary space."

He walks around to stand in front of me. I look up at him waiting for him to speak. He keeps looking at me and finally leans down and gives me a hug. It's not something new, but it's a bit rare. I kiss him on the jaw as he stands up. Without another word I walk into my room and shut the door.

THIRTEEN

I wake up to someone knocking on my bedroom door. This is not necessarily an unusual occurrence but with the way things are going, I'm afraid something has happened to Kenny or Leo. Not to mention the guys at the desks should have stopped whoever it was from getting this far into my flat. I decide I need to know what's going on before I open the door. I yell at whoever is on the other side, "What's wrong?"

I hear Eric's voice through the door. "Boss, Cane is here and I'm fairly sure he's having an issue with tomorrow's dress code."

I put a pillow over my face and scream. "Someone call Jacob for breakfast or lunch or whatever meal is appropriate. I'll be out, after a shower."

I find the three delinquents and Jack sitting around my large dining table. There's more chatting than eating occurring, but I much prefer it to all of them sitting around in awkward silence. I walk up behind Kenny's wheelchair and whisper in his ear, "Do you have a note saying you can be up here?"

He sits up straighter in his chair. I think I caught him off guard with the whispering. He probably counted on me yelling. I walk around to the side of his chair, so I can get a good look at him. I put my hand out and say, "Well?"

"In my own defense," Kenny says, "the doc said not to get too excited. The whole ninja whispering sexy thing you did is making my sweat pants a bit less loose fitting."

He's looking up at me, the entire time he's speaking, with a slight hint of his damn joker grin. I give him a raised eyebrow and take my seat at the table.

I put food on my plate while Jack pours me some mystery juice. "What the hell is this?" I swish it around in the glass and give it a sniff.

"Don't know. It came with the tray. I would assume it has lots of healthy things in it." Jack drinks a bit from his glass and only makes a minor face of distaste. Of course, you can't fry juice, so Jack is only so helpful when it comes to giving a useful opinion on healthy food.

"Okay, so I got out of bed because apparently Cane, you have some issue with tomorrow's attire. What's the problem?" I put ketchup on my scrambled eggs waiting for an answer.

"It's simple. I don't have a suit." He has a look on his face like someone forgot to invite him to the party.

I finish chewing before asking, "You had fancy clothes when you picked me up from the airport. Are those the only clothes Donna gave you?"

"Yea, I don't have a full suit and if you recall the shirt got blood on it."

I turn to Jack, "When are the fittings?"

He chews and talks at the same time because he's feral. "Jacob said he'd be ready after we eat."

"Cane, everyone here has dress clothes. I'm sure it's on your to-do list. It so happens we need a bit sooner than planned. All you guys put on and takeoff weight so often most of you require at least three suits. Hell, some of them have several because they like to dress fancy when they aren't working. We have a few who will get fitted for new ones along with you today. We don't do trendy styles. If you desire something trendy, *you* pay for it, but you don't wear it on jobs or with me in public, *ever*. The suits we pay for will accommodate your weapons and let's face it; I want to look at what I want to look at."

Kenny pipes in, "Brother, I recommend you go with what she picks. I tried to pick my own stuff when I got my first suits. I looked like my mother dressed me for school pictures. I even went out dressed in said clothes and girls asked me if I had lost my mommy. It was humiliating. So, I quickly apologized to the boss and asked for her choice. Next time I went out, I wasn't alone for too many nights." There was no containing the laughter at the table after his last proclamation.

When I finish eating I push the call button on the table top phone. I tell Jacob we're ready when he is. Jack gets on his phone. He tells whoever is on the other end it's time to grab everyone who needs suits. Five minutes later Jacob appears with Drew pushing a large wardrobe.

Eric and Jack move the large dining table against the window, so Jacob can lay out his things. This also clears out a huge spot where Drew can place the dressing platform for the guys to stand on. Drew also pulls a long-standing mirror from the back of the coat closet and sets it near the small platform.

There's a knock on the door and Eric answers it. Three guys walk in and I tell Jacob they need to go first since they just need to up-date their measurements. They take their turns and head back to work. I motion for Eric to get up on the square. He looks at me a little confused.

"Don't look at me as if I'm crazy. I know for a fact

you need a new suit, and this is a good reason. So, get your ass up there."

He sighs, shrugs his shoulders in resignation and gets up on the step. Jacob begins to take measurements and speaks to Drew in some tailoring language I don't speak.

Drew hands Eric a pair of pants from the wardrobe along with a shirt as Eric strips down to his under bits. Of course, the three stooges start to clap and throw money on the ground. Eric does his best to ignore them. I'm glad he has underwear on, given last night's commando show.

Once Eric has everything on Jacob starts to mark things up as well as pinning anyplace which needs it. Once he finishes he turns to me. "Miss, if you would please."

I get up and walk around to make sure everything looks like it should. "I like it. Now Eric, all you need to do is choose a color." Drew hands him his clothes as well as the money thrown on the floor. Drew says something to him none of us can hear. Eric shakes his hand and takes a seat next to Kenny who is enjoying the show from his wheelchair.

"Okay Cane, you're up." I motion for him to get on the platform. He steps up and Jacob once again takes the needed measurements.

Jacob tells Drew what he needs, and Cane realizes it's his turn to disrobe. As he does, the other three start throwing money but add whistling this time. Cane puts on the pants and shirt without comment.

Jacob does his thing and finally motions for me to come over. "Miss, I do believe we are going to have to make him a custom shirt. I don't have anything already on hand suitable given his neck, arm and waist measurements."

I get up on the platform with him to get a better look at the parts of the shirt Jacob is talking about. I can quickly see what he means. I nod and pull the shirt taut at the waist as I lean back to see what I can see. "Drew, can I have a vest please?"

Drew retrieves a few different styles from the wardrobe and brings them over.

I hand them to Cane one at a time, taking time with each one to see which one looks best. I find the one where the top button sits at mid sternum. "Jacob, I think given his waist we need to add a vest. I think it will look very handsome."

Jacob smiles and agrees.

Drew is standing by with the large sections of different kinds of cloth in several of my favorite colors. I hold them up to Cane "Okay, I want this done in the very dark black herringbone. Drew, let Cane pick whichever fabric he likes best. Please make sure it's weather appropriate."

Jacob writes everything down.

Drew packs everything back into the wardrobe and Jacob waves me over to look at his drawings. "Miss, I think this would look best. I wanted to get your approval before I get started, especially with the shirt."

Jacob's drawing is amazing and spot on as always. "I think for tomorrow the shirt should be done in pewter." I turn and let Cane know he will need to be available as he will be required to make sure everything fits.

He nods his understanding as he puts his clothes back on.

I point a finger at Jack. "Make sure to call the cage. Remind everyone shoulder holsters are to be worn and weapons loaded tomorrow. Also make sure they're clear about the dress code." He nods and gives me a mock salute.

"I'm going to spend the rest of the day in my office. Jack, call me when your stone guy gets here." He waves at me as he follows Jacob and Drew out the front door.

I hear Eric and Kenny chatting about picking out a suit for Patrick. They pull Cane into the conversation by asking him if he would help them with some design ideas on Eric's new extra-large space. I leave them there and take the back stairs to my office.

I fill the rest of the day with emails, phone calls, and answering questions about the memorial service.

As the sun starts to set Jacob enters my office quietly and waits patiently for me to finish the call I'm on. I hang up and look at him.

"Miss, Jack asked me to tell you the stone mason is here, and they are waiting for you at the kitchen delivery bay. I, however, was on my way to ask you about dinner."

I think about it for a minute. "Go ahead and make some family style dishes and send out a message all are invited. Depending on the reply set it up in the appropriate space."

He nods and leaves to make the arrangements.

I log off my computer and decide to use the back stairs to meet Jack. I don't want to get sidetracked by going through the public areas. I reach the part of the kitchen where the deliveries come in and I walk to the back where the big roll-up doors are. I find Jack and his stone guy chatting and smoking.

"So, am I going to have to hang the slab myself?"

Edward turns to me and smiles. He puts his cigarette out and punches Jack in the arm. "You knew she was there, didn't you?"

Jack takes one last pull off his disgusting imported cigarette and laughs. "I would like to say I did, but she *is* very stealthy when she wants to be."

Edward walks over, picks me up and gives me a hug. After he's done squeezing me, he gently sets me back on my feet. He takes a moment to look at me and then whistles through his teeth.

I look towards the rolling doors and his foreman is directing his crew of fifteen. He is pointing out to them, using the map on his tablet, where the equipment needs to go. I recognize the guys walking past me. It can take forever for us to vet the security backgrounds of our contract workers, so once we find ones we like we always use them, besides Jack *always* knows someone.

Jack walks up next to me and puts his arm around my shoulder as I put my arm around his waist. We follow the workers to the main lobby in silence. Jack and I have not had to do this too many times, but we always agreed things like this should be done at night with no audience. The workers set up lights and cover the large windows. Jack walks to the large wall and scratches his beard. I take a step behind one of the lights. I can feel the tears running down my face and I prefer to be alone, in the dark, with my thoughts.

Jack doesn't turn around. "Alex, I think we should

put it right here in the center behind the desk. What do you think?" The sound of his voice shaking is breaking my heart.

I walk around the light and stand about a foot behind him. I know he knows I'm there. I take a deep breath before answering him. "I think the center is good, but I think we should put it up high. He would have liked the view from up there." He nods and hangs his head.

Jack clears his throat. "Well, Edward, you heard the lady. Put it up top and center it." He turns and without really looking at me he kisses me on the cheek and leaves me standing in lobby.

Edward and his workers simply go to work without a word. I appreciate their silence more than the fact they agreed to work through the night. I stand there, arms crossed, watching them as they work much like Eric sat with Patrick's body the first night. At some point someone brought me a blanket, Jacob I'm assuming. I pull it tight around myself, but I continue to watch the men carefully hang and secure the giant slab. Once they start the final polish, I pull a stack of cash from my pocket. I thank Edward and pay him before I leave the room. I know Jacob is watching somewhere and will make sure they are escorted back to their vehicles.

I get on the elevator and lean against the side, so I don't lay down on the floor and go to sleep. I wave at the guys at the desks as I walk past them. I still have the blanket wrapped around me as I climb into bed, clothes and all.

FOURTEEN

I feel someone in my space, but I can't tell if it's part of a dream or real life barging in. I can barely hear someone talking to me. "Miss, it is time to wake up. I have set out your clothes."

I untangle myself from the sheets and without a word I go to the bathroom and shut the door. I take more time than usual today. I need to make sure my facade is shiny; it will keep all the crap on the inside from spilling out. It's the best plan I have. I exit the bathroom and Jacob has hung up three pant suits.

Now, I know it's traditional to wear modest clothes to a funeral. However, I think it's important to say goodbye to your friend in an outfit they would have liked seeing you in. Therefore, I choose the pant suit with a vest. The kicker about this choice is, there is no top worn under the vest. Patrick was a boob man and I decide this is clearly the only option for my final goodbye to him. I put on my shoulder holster. It's currently empty but I know Jack will bring my HK with him.

Jacob knocks and enters the room with my shoes in his hand. "Miss, I have polished these for you."

I smile as I take them from him and set them on the floor. Once I'm put together Jacob takes a final look and helps me with my jacket since it goes over my gear. He makes a few adjustments and then smiles at me.

"Miss, Mr. Sterling is waiting for you in the living room."

I thank him quietly and open the door.

Jack is standing by the large table still pushed against the far wall from the night before. He's looking out the windows, but turns when he hears my heels clicking on the floor. He smiles, "Well, don't you look fancy." As expected he has my HK in his hand. I walk over and open my jacket, so he can put it in the holster for me.

We both turn when we hear a knock at the door. Jacob is quick to his duties. When he opens it, Eric is standing on the other side all dressed up. I smile at him as he walks in.

Jacob exits without a word, leaving Jack, Eric and me alone.

Eric shakes Jack's hand and then looks at me. "Patrick *was* a boob man. Great choice, boss." I punch him, and he smiles rubbing his arm. Eric looks around the room. "I thought Cane would be up here already."

Jack was the one with the answer. "Kenny asked him to be a pallbearer, so they're seeing to things."

Some of the tension seems to leave Eric's shoulders at hearing this bit of news. I know he trusts Kenny and it's good to see Cane has earned a special spot with the two of them.

I hear Jack's phone beep. He looks at it, sends a short reply and then turns the phone off. "Everything is ready. Eric, when you're ready we can go down."

Eric stands up straight and reaches out his hand to me. I don't say a thing, I take his hand and we start towards the door. I can hear Jack's boots behind us. We get on the elevator and ride down to the lobby in silence.

When the doors open I can see Jacob and his staff were hard at work last night.

Eric leans down and whispers, "Patrick would have hated all this fuss, but he would've loved the way this looks."

I look up at him and wink.

Jack makes a clicking sound and we both turn to see seven of Patrick's team mates along with Cane carrying the flag draped coffin on their shoulders. Kenny, as he was restricted to the wheelchair, is in front of the casket leading the procession. Cane and I make eye contact and he nods ever so slightly. I feel a nudge in my ribs and look down to see Jack was nice enough to bring me a pair of black sunglasses.

As the casket turns the corner I hear the music start. It's Jimi Hendrix' *Star Spangled Banner*. I hear the dress shoes tap on the floor as all the men stand up and salute the casket as it makes its way down the center aisle. Most of these guys are former military, in some way or another, and they get all the bells and whistles for their service.

Once the casket has been set down on the high dais under the covered piece of marble, Cane, Kenny and the others join the rest of us. Jerome, as our in-house doctor and spiritual mentor, takes care of the service. He speaks from the heart for a short time and then asks if anyone has anything else they would like to share. When no one stands he asks for a moment of silence. He thanks everyone and we all lift our heads.

Jerome motions to Kenny. He wheels himself off to the side and at the same time Eric as well as Patrick's other team mates stand up. Eric calls the men to attention and the entire room stands up in unison. Eric gives his commands for the Twenty-one-gun salute. The seven men draw their side arms load their magazines, which contain blanks, and fire three times in unison. Kenny picks up the bugle from his lap, pauses to collect himself and then starts to play *Taps*. It gets me every fucking time. We all stand in silence as other members of Patrick's team fold the flag draped over his coffin. The flag is presented to Eric as he was Patrick's closest friend.

Jerome asks everyone to have a seat. "At this time, I will turn it over to Jack and Alex." Jack grabs my hand and we walk up to the raised podium overlooking the room.

Jack squeezes my hand and I start to speak. "We don't like to lose a member of our family, but we all know it is not a case of *if* but *when*. The important thing to remember is if we keep them in our hearts they are never truly gone. We would like to unveil Patrick's memorial stone."

Jack turns to Jerome and he pulls the cord. The black draping flutters to the floor revealing the beautifully polished blood marble.

I notice Eric starting to come apart. I also see, as brothers should, Cane and Kenny are at his side.

Jack addresses the group. "In an hour there will be a proper party taking place in the largest banquet room. Attendance is not mandatory, but I think we all know Patrick would have wanted us all to be together to celebrate his life." When Jack finishes we walk down the steps and he pauses.

We walk over to the casket; Jack salutes and knocks twice. I kiss the cold wood and knock twice before stepping back. We walk over to Eric and Kenny. Jack and I hug them both. I lean over to Cane. "Stay with them until everyone is gone."

"I will." He says, kissing my cheek.

Jack and I get on the elevator and go back upstairs to change. When I get to my room Jacob is there laying out clothes. He has chosen comfortable jeans and one of my favorite wrestling shirts. I thank him before I sit down at the dressing table to refresh my makeup. It won't last, but I must make the effort.

"Miss, I thought the service was very nice," he says, putting my heels away.

"I agree. Is the banquet room ready?"

"The room, as well as the food, is ready and waiting."

I nod at his statement.

"Miss, are we waiting on the cremation, or is it to take place as soon as the gentlemen are done downstairs?"

I turn to him. "Honestly?" I've nothing left to answer the question. "Please ask Jack. I think Eric and the rest of their team will want to be there, but Jack will need to take care of it."

Before I can say anything else I hear Jack yelling from the living room. "Alex, are you dressed?"

"Yeah, almost! Hey, Jacob needs to talk to you. I'll be out in a few."

He doesn't say anything in reply, so Jacob leaves my room to speak to him.

I finish changing clothes and find Jack sitting at the dining table with a full glass of brown liquid sitting in front of him. "What are you drinking?" I nod at the glass.

"Gentleman Jack."

"It was Patrick's favorite." It was a statement not a question.

Jack raises the glass and takes a drink.

I smile at him and sit down in the chair next to him. We sit their holding hands as he drinks.

"What did you tell Jacob about the cremation?"

Jack takes another long drink before answering. "I told him we would wait so the team could be there."

I squeeze his hand because words aren't necessary at this point. We sit there in silence for a while before a knock at the door brings us both around.

Jack yells for whoever it is to come in.

The door opens and in walks Cane with Eric pushing Kenny. All three of them have cleaned up and changed their clothes.

Eric pulls out a chair, so Kenny has a place to slide into. Cane takes a seat next to me and Eric takes a seat next to Jack.

Jack is the first to speak, "I've set the cremation for tomorrow morning, so your entire team can be there. If you think another time would be better, let me know."

Eric takes Jack's glass and finishes his drink. "Thanks, I appreciate it. I agree tomorrow morning is best. I'll send a message to the team."

The alarm on Jack's watch goes off.

"Okay gentlemen, it's time to go downstairs." I say this as I walk past Cane gripping his shoulder. Everyone pushes away from the table and heads for the door. We all ride down to the banquet room together, in silence.

The banquet doors are open, and Jacob is giving instructions to his staff. They appear to be unloading enough food to feed a third world country. With the oversized doors open, I get a panoramic view of the space. Most of the guys are already sitting at the large tables. They're not eating yet, which I'm sure is taking all the restraint they can muster.

Jack, Cane, Eric and Kenny go in and pick a table to occupy. I'm still in the doorway watching them. None of them are talking to each other. They're mostly ogling the food. I sense there's someone behind me. When I look over my shoulder I see the remainder of the teams standing behind me, waiting patiently.

"Don't let me stop you," I turn sideways and wave them into the room.

They quickly move past me and fill the remaining seats.

Jacob comes and stands next to me. "Miss, things are ready when you are."

"Have at it gentlemen!" I say motioning towards the buffet. There's the collective sound of chairs sliding across the wood floor. I look at Jacob with my eyebrow raised. "I don't see any nachos." I say a bit loudly since some of the guys have started to chat among themselves. He points towards the table where Jack is sitting.

I see Drew standing next to a cart with a fancy silver covered tray, like the ones in the movies. Kenny tries to lift the lid, but Drew stops him. Cane leans in and says something to him. Kenny turns around to look at me and yells, "Boss, your nachos are here!"

I grin at both Jacob and Kenny. As I start for the table I see Drew take the plate from under the silver lid. I take my seat between Cane and Jack as Drew puts the hot plate of cheesy goodness in front of me. "In the words of *Hell Boy*, 'Mmmmm Nachos'," I say as I stuff a few chips into my face.

Drew quietly pushes the cart back to the open doors. Jacob and the rest of his staff make their way out, kind enough to quietly and politely close the doors behind themselves.

I look around and notice none of the TV's are on. I yell across the room, "Kevin, how come none of the TV's are on?" I smile as I see him jump a little in his seat.

He takes another drink of his beer before answering. "Boss, I'm testing some new stuff. Touch the space to the right of your water glass. I've replaced part of the table top with a remote." He takes another drink of his beer.

I wave at him to let him know I heard him. "Well hell, this is going to be interesting." I say, mostly to myself. I reach out, do as I was instructed. Sure, as shit the glass top on the table comes to life. The blue outline of a remote appears.

I touch the ON button on the remote display and the TV's turn on. *Nice*. I touch the DVR button on the display. When my list appears on the screens I choose the 2015 Rugby World Cup Final match. I mean, who doesn't want to watch history being made, again. The guys carefully tap their beer bottles and glasses on the tables in approval. Once I take my hand away the blue light along with the remote display disappears.

Cane leans over to me as the national anthems are about to start, "I guess sex on this table is out of the question."

Eric, who was sitting to his left, almost swallows

his face. I laughed as much at him as I did about Cane's comment. I wink at Cane and he grins.

Jacob and his staff continue to come in and out of the room like elves at Christmas. They take away the dirty plates and clean ones take their place. As the trays of food are emptied they are replaced with more food. The men and I continue to eat, drink and cheer the game like we did when we saw it in England. Maybe a little more now, since our excitement had to be contained because we were working the first time. At about the sixty-minute mark in the game the plates begin to disappear and no more take their places. The trays of food stop coming, and the emptied ones are removed.

Jacob leaves digestion enabling liquors on each of the tables. I don't partake in any of them, but a lot of the guys like them. As the match comes to an end the banquet doors open wide and the guys slowly make their way out into the hallway. I'm sure Drew is out there to make sure those who have honored Patrick a bit too much are safely directed to their flats to sleep it off.

Eric sees Kenny on the verge of sleep and lets us know he will take him back to his medical suite. "Boss, I'm going to stay with Kenny tonight."

I rise and kiss Kenny and Eric on the cheek.

Kenny giggles and Eric smiles as he turns to push his friend out of the room.

Jack gets up from his seat and takes one more pull from his beer. He kisses me at the temple and reaches out to shake Cane's hand. Without any words he leaves the room as well.

As the interviews and the post victory festivities continue, Cane and I sit and enjoy the emptiness of the room. I feel Cane sit up quickly next to me; he's heard something I didn't. I look over at him knowing this can't be good. "I am *not* working today. So, whoever it is needs to go away."

Cane holds his hand up, "I hear quick boots coming." I put my head down on the table, in the universal sign of, *'Oh for fucks sake'*.

"Boss", says a breathless voice from the doorway.

"Is someone dead? Because you should not even be on this floor much less in this room if someone is not dead."

"Boss, Corey dented your truck," the voice says.

I say again, "Is *someone* dead?"

"Son," Cane says, trying not to laugh, "is Corey dead, or did he hit a person who then died?"

The young man at the door has caught his breath. "Boss, I was told to come and tell you Corey damaged your truck. I don't know the circumstances."

I wave my hands in surrender. "Ok, I'm on my way." I get up and before Cane can get up I rub my hands over my face, turn and give him the eye. "If you make me go down there alone, I will make sure Jacob doesn't have any more chocolate brownie cake for you."

I hear the chair push away from the table as he laughs softly. "You're mean. You know his cake has healing properties."

We get on the elevator and Cane hits the button. When the doors open into the garage there is a lot of commotion. "You should have put better shoes on." Cane says under his breath looking down at my three stripe slides. What Cane still hasn't realized, is this garage is usually clean enough for me to eat off the floor.

If it isn't, someone is going to lose their job and perhaps a limb especially if I step on something other than concrete.

"Ramone," I yell across the garage. "Ramone, what the hell happened to my truck?" I yell a bit louder into the empty space.

As my voice gets louder some of the mechanics start to find things to do in the far corners of the large space. Ramone starts towards me and waves his hand at my truck. I can see Corey is currently sitting on the clearly broken running board.

"Corey," I fix my eyes on him and he looks away, "*what* did you do to my truck and even more important; what in the fuck were you doing driving my truck?"

Corey stands up, "Boss, I only took your truck because it was closest to the door and they were detailing the one I usually use, again. They missed some spots the first time. Anyway, we got a line on the pervert who's been hanging around some of the schools."

I turn, and Ramone is flipping him off, I'm sure because of the detailing comment. I look at Cane and bless him, he's trying to keep a straight face. I turn back to face Corey. "Let me see if I understand. The story is: pervert possibly located, your truck has spots, and my truck was closest. Do I have this right?"

Corey looks at me as if I'm the one who lacks comprehension skills. I can hear Cane counting behind me. I'm not sure if it's for him or me, but either way it's currently keeping me from stabbing Corey with any random sharp object I can put my hands on.

"What was the result of this little adventure?" I

shove my hands in my pockets more for this idiot's safety than anything else.

"Okay, so we got the call and I gathered my team. I knew I needed to take charge because of what was going on today. We got down here, and I saw the truck wasn't ready. I grabbed the keys to your truck since it was closest and ready. I found the pervert right where the tech geeks told us he would be. Of course, it's my luck he crosses the street as my support team was going to grab him on the opposite side of the road. We approached from the other direction, but the guy stops on the island in the middle waiting for traffic to pass. I had Kimble slow down. I opened the door and I stretched out the back window. I grabbed him by his shirt and slammed him against the door." He gestures at my truck. "Which is how the…uh…dent occurred."

I know Cane is standing at my back. I turn around and I rest my head on Cane's shoulder. When I turn around Cane's 9mm in my hand and I fire three quick shots into the floor at Corey's feet. I hand the weapon back to Cane. He takes it and puts it back in the rear of his waistband where I got it from.

"Who has a phone?" I ask.

Kimble hands me his phone and it's already ringing.

"Jack, get down to the garage," is all I say before hanging up.

I tell Ramone to get me a new truck and to call the wrecker to take my burnt out one away. It only takes Jack a few minutes to bang his way into the garage from the stairwell.

"What the hell happened here?" Jack yells. "I only left you alone for five minutes."

Cane is the only one who says anything. "He bounced a pervert off her truck and then made it sound like he did it all alone. To add to the heap of steaming fuck he made it sound like she should be grateful he took care of it."

Jack walks over and looks at Corey, the wet spot spreading between his legs where he pissed himself. It's draining onto the floor. He bends over at the waist, hands on his knees, and starts to laugh. He looks back at me, "Well I'm not cleaning *this* up."

When Jack turns back around I nudge Cane and we take off for the elevator. We don't say anything all the way back up to my flat. The doors open, and my watchmen stand up as we exit. They look over my shoulder at Cane.

"He's here to make sure I don't shoot anyone else with his gun." I tell them.

They both nod and unlock my doors.

Cane nods and leaves his weapon with Waylon, "If you could put the three bullets back she used, I would appreciate it."

I laugh at the remark and continue to the couch. I find the remote and turn the TV on, deciding watching Netflix is the way to finish this day. I can hear the TV, but I can also hear someone snoring and I'm pretty sure it's not me. I look around and Cane is asleep on the other part of the giant L-shaped couch. Apparently, the buffet, the shooting, and Netflix worked as a giant fuzzy sleeping pill.

*****

At some point I must have joined Cane in sleep, on my own section of the couch. When I wake I'm not sure what time it is since I don't have any clocks near the TV. Jacob has pulled the night shades in the room, but it only means I'm asleep. It doesn't always indicate the time of day.

I try to locate my phone. After a bit of flopping about and not finding it; I notice a small flashing blue light in the glass sculpture on the coffee table. I don't remember how it got there, but there it is none the less. Swinging my legs around, I can sense someone is watching me. I look over and notice Cane is awake, but he doesn't say anything. It dawns on me as I reach for my phone the coffee table is ridiculously huge.

"Who the fuck bought this giant damn table; a person can't even reach the center without laying on it," I say, not really expecting an answer.

Cane chuckles as I lay across the table to reach the phone. I don't even bother trying to get off the table before I look at it. I simply prop myself up on my elbows and push the buttons on the side of the phone until it comes to life. The phone display shows me it's a little after two in the morning. Insomnia sucks *so hard.*

"What time is it?" Cane asks.

I flail my arm towards him with the phone in my hand, so he can see the display.

"Not helpful." He grunts as he sits up. He takes the phone and looks at it.

I lay flat on the table and contemplate getting up.

"Are you stuck?" he asks.

"No…just not terribly interested in moving."

He laughs and clears his throat. "Well it's two in the morning. Would you like me to go? I can only imagine what the watch dogs must be thinking."

I scoot off the table and flop onto the floor. "First of all, the guard dogs don't get paid to think about what goes on behind the doors unless it concerns my safety. Second, we had probably one of the best naps ever so attempting to go back to sleep now would be a waste of time. Third, if you want to go, feel free. If you want to stick around it's okay too. I'm going to brush my teeth and go down and check on my new truck. If you wanna' join me, you know where the extra bathroom is, help yourself."

I go into the bathroom and I can hear Cane rise as his boots thud across the room. I change into clean clothes as my other ones have remnants of the earlier buffet on them and head back out to the main room. Cane is in the kitchen getting something to drink and looks far more awake then he did a few minutes ago. I nod towards the door and he pulls it open as both of the men on the other side stand up.

There is one of the building's exterior guards standing at Derek's desk. He looks me up and down and says, "Have we changed our clothes?"

I notice he isn't really talking to anyone. I raise my eyebrow in question. "Is there a reason why you are inside the building? Better yet, what the fuck are you doing on this floor?"

Cane has stopped and extends his hand to Waylon at the other desk to get his weapon back. "At this rate I'm going to need three more bullets," he tells Waylon before returning the weapon to the small of his back.

The guard looks at me with some confusion. "I was dropping off Derek's keys. He let me borrow his car on my lunch break."

I look over at Derek and he nods. "Boss, I apologize. I didn't want to leave my post to get my keys back. I now realize I could have had him leave the keys with Ramone."

"Are you done dropping off the keys?" I ask the guard.

"Yes ma'am. I'm headed back outside now." He says without regret or apology. He walks to the stairwell without another word.

Cane nudges me, "You're going to have him cutting the dog park grass with manicure scissors, aren't you?"

I punch him in the arm and jump on the elevator. When we reach the garage, it smells like birthday cake and burnt rubber. This tells me Jacob has made sure someone knew their birthday wasn't forgotten, even with all the crap we've been going through today. Also, it tells me my damaged truck has been taken care of.

"Ramone," I yell.

He walks out from under a McLaren on a lift on the other side of the room. "Woman, why are you yellin'?" he asks with a grin on his face.

We make our way over to him, "I'm yelling because it's only slightly louder than a rock concert in here." I say as one of several impact wrenches goes off somewhere.

"Your truck was sick with moron cooties, so I had

to put it down. However, I made a call and we have procured another one, even with the late hour." He points over my shoulder to a brand-new truck being worked on in the corner.

"Ramone," I gaze at my new truck, "I want a retina scanner or DNA or *whatever* installed so some fool can't take my truck again without permission."

Ramone laughs, "Way ahead of you, boss."

"Good, now we have all of this mess out of the way, I think Cane here needs a company car as well. Please get with him sometime this week and find out what he wants." Ramone nods and I walk away before Cane can object.

I walk to the elevator with Cane following and I push the button for the kitchen. Cane cusses as he has to quick step to try to catch up to me. I lean against the back wall and wait for him. The doors start to close, and Cane shoves his arm between the doors to stop them. Instead of getting into the elevator he stands legs wide on the threshold, so the doors can't close at all. He stands there long enough to set the alarm off.

I continue to lean against the wall and wait for him to figure out what he's going to do. I wave my hand and Cane takes a second to look over his shoulder. He now sees two guys with their weapons out standing behind him. The alarm has sounded long enough the security detail on the garage level responded. Cane rubs both of his hands over his face and steps inside the elevator. The alarm shuts off as he gets out of the way. I wave at the security detail as the doors close.

"I don't want a company car. If you give me a vehicle it will sit in the garage and collect dust," Cane tells me in one long breath. He stands next to me at the back of the elevator with his arms crossed over his chest.

I shrug. "First of all, Ramone would cut off his own pecker before he would let any of the transportation become dusty. Second, the car is for your everyday travel when you are not with me or Jack. It's to be used when you wander to your storage unit or who knows where, you may at some point go on a date. Hell, you may want to escape the madness and go to a strip club." He starts to speak, but I hold up my hand to silence him. "You can't take one of the work trucks out for everyday stuff. Get with Ramone and pick something out."

The doors open at the kitchen level and Cane and I take the hallway to the right. At the end I see Jacob. I'm sure at some level he's judging me, but he's going to feed me anyway.

I know Jacob likes to say things like, *'You know you should probably work out both AM and PM tomorrow.'* He's such an asshole sometimes. He's not wrong but, *whatever*.

"Miss, are you looking for a late-night snack or an early morning snack?" he says in his proper butler voice. I always find it most interesting he's always dressed properly no matter what time of the day or night it is. I'm sure he sleeps in the damn outfit.

"Jacob, I would like something in a donut," I walk past him into the kitchen. Cane isn't sure what to do, but he follows me.

"And you, sir?" Jacob looks at Cane.

"I'm making sure no one kills her, and she doesn't choke to death on whatever she is about to eat."

Jacob laughs at this. "I wish you luck with both of those tasks."

The counters and surfaces are clean and there are no workers anywhere, but Jacob can still manage to produce what I want to eat. I suspect he keeps emergency stock for occasions like this. I take a seat at one of the high work stations and Cane takes a seat across from me. Jacob appears with a tray and on it are all the things I usually want this time of night.

Cane has a look on his face I can only described as sugar shock.

Jacob puts the tray down along with two large cold bottles of water and walks away.

Cane laughs, "Is this usual for your after-hour's meal?"

I stuff part of a bear claw with melted butter into my mouth and nod at him.

He shakes his head and takes a piece of birthday cake off the tray. He picks up his fork and starts to laugh again.

I look over at him. "What's so funny?" I say past the mouthful of food.

He points at the cake. I look at his piece and start to laugh. The piece he chose has writing on it, it says Eugene. "Do you think your butler killed Eugene and took his birthday cake or did he walk into a child's birthday party and take it?"

I laugh almost hard enough to shoot bear claw out my nose. "Jacob would never take cake from a kid." Cane starts laughing and I'm pretty sure he hasn't laughed this hard in a while. We help ourselves to a few more desserts and make our way up the stairs to the residential floors.

As we exit I notice there are no extra people standing outside my doors. I nod at Waylon and he returns the gesture.

"You need to have a car chosen before the end of the day." I say as I make my way to my room.

"Yes, Ma'am," is all I hear as the TV turns on. I don't even bother asking him why he isn't going back to his own room. I grin to myself as I shut the bedroom door.

FIFTEEN

Two Months Later…

I'm pretty sure I didn't hear an alarm but I'm awake anyway. This means one of two things. One, I forgot to set the alarm during one of my insomnia episodes last night. Or two: Jacob came in and turned off the alarm because clearly, I wasn't getting up. Either way I need to find out what time it is. I slap at the side table until I feel my phone. I open one eye; the display reads nine-fifteen a.m. *Well, it could be worse, I guess.*

I get up and go through all the bathroom motions. I choose comfortable clothes, but work clothes none the less. I mean it's not like the people I see will be offended if I have jeans on with a shirt saying, *'Go Fuck a Toad'.* If they don't like it, they are free to go elsewhere. I know they aren't going anywhere and so do they. I pick up my steel-toe boots and go out to the kitchen.

As soon as I open the door I can smell bacon and fresh bread, sourdough I think. In my kitchen area, Jack, Cane and Kenny are sitting at the table. It has been a couple of months since Patrick's death and things are getting back to normal. Kenny has been out of the wheel-chair for a little over a month and is almost back to one hundred percent.

Jack is reading from a stack of brown and red report folders. Cane is watching the TV over the fireplace.

Kenny is eating peacefully and playing on his phone.

"Well it's about time you got the hell out here. You know your creepy butler will not feed any of us until he knows you'll be out soon?" Jack says loudly, without looking up from his reading.

Cane turns his head in my direction and winks. Kenny nods.

"Well you appear to be eating so I'm confused as to why you're bitching."

Cane's shoulders shake in quiet laughter. Kenny gives me a thumbs-up over his head.

Jack picks up a piece of bacon from his plate. "Laugh it up you bastards. Wait until you sit here for three hours waiting for breakfast while princess insomnia over there gets her beauty sleep." Jack shakes the piece of bacon at Cane.

Cane snatches the bacon out of Jack's hand and eats it. "I'd just go to the kitchen and get food. If you're waiting for her then you don't want to get your own food. I'm guessing with your brittle bones you don't want to have to walk the buffet line with the guys. I'm sure Jacob can get you an elder pass to cut the line if it would help."

Jack for all his effort can't fight it and starts to laugh.

I take a seat next to Cane, so I can see the TV and I fill my plate with bacon and a couple of sourdough mini-bagels.

Cane grabs the chilled pitcher of orange juice from the counter and fills a glass for all of us.

There's a knock at the door. Jack raises his hand and gets up to open the door. It's Eric and he has several folders under his arm and he's reading something on his tablet. Eric has recovered as much as anyone can from the loss of a brother. I think the completion of his new expanded flat helps.

"Morning, is she awake?" Eric asks without looking up.

"Yes, *she* is," I say.

Eric looks up. "Hey, sorry, I have some guys for you to look at for the still vacant perimeter security post and some ops team vacancies."

I nod my head and hold out my hand because by this time I've shoved more food in my face. He walks towards me and hands me the folders.

"Do you have some front runners?" I open them all up on the table in the space Cane has cleared. Eric starts to fill up a plate for himself as I begin to quickly discard some of the choices.

"To answer your question, those are the only ones Jack and I felt would be suitable." Eric pours himself some coffee.

I return to reading the files. I stop cold, mouth open. I'm almost sure some bacon fell out. "Is this a woman? What the hell is a woman doing on our payroll? I mean, hell, I know we did a lot of cleaning house, but I thought we still had plenty of candidates to choose from." The room, even with the TV on, is suddenly eerily quiet.

Jack clears his throat. "She's not on the payroll, *yet*. She's an outside prospect I felt we could discuss, you know, like adults. I know your feeling on this subject but read the report and we can talk about it," he says on a long exhale.

"Guys, we need the room," I say sharply.

Kenny picks up his plate as Cane motions toward the back staircase leading to his flat. Eric picks up his plate and follows the two of them through the door.

"Alright old man let's hear your reasons why I should even entertain the ridiculous idea of hiring this woman for an ops team," I ask, probably a bit loud.

"A buddy called. She's been working in secret with the various branches. She wants to get out of the life and into the private sector. The good news is she doesn't want to crawl around in the dirt anymore, but she does want the potential to get to shoot people."

I look at him as if he has lost his mind. I'm almost positive my eyebrows have disappeared into my hair.

"The *answer* is no." I close her file and put it in the reject pile.

"You won't even meet her?" he asks.

"Not only no, but *fuck no.*" I stuff more bacon in my face, mostly out of sheer annoyance. I finish my juice, put my boots on and head to the stairs to go to my office. I leave Jack sitting in my flat without saying another word.

*****

I spend most of the day in my office alone. I'm not taking calls, but I am returning some of my messages. I sift through my emails and check on the progress of any of the teams in the field. I know Jacob has come in and out a few times because my tea continues to be replenished and hot. I have started a list of items I need to cover and who I need to cover them with. I have not, however, figured out what I'm going to do about the perimeter employee situation. I mean it took a few months to get the guy who previously held the job to give notice. He finally got tired of being assigned the shit jobs after being on my floor without permission. At this point I may get some gun towers and call it a day.

I realize I'm no longer alone in the room. I look up and in front of me stands Jacob with his hands clasped behind his back.

"Yes?" I ask as I raise my eyebrow in question.

He hands me an invoice. This is odd because Jacob knows they go to the accountants. I take it from him and read over it.

"What the fresh hell kind of furniture repair costs $4,000?" I look at Jacob with what I'm sure is bewilderment.

"Miss, it is the cost for the boardroom table you used as a butcher block." Jacob never loses his cool even when he probably should.

"The table didn't even *cost* that much!"

"Miss, the original cost of the table was $27,000."

I am still completely confused. He simply continues. "With the original cost, the repair price is more than reasonable."

I notice there are pages attached to the invoice. I skim over them and begin to understand the amount of work it will take to return the table to its original condition. I begin to feel bad for stabbing the table. I sign the invoice and hand it back to Jacob. "Clearly the craftsmanship is worth the cost."

I notice Jacob is still standing in front of my desk. I sigh. "Is there more?"

"Yes, Miss. Mr. Radford has suggested we should purchase one of the steel top table designs if accidents like this are likely to happen again. He's stated they would be easier to repair and harder to damage."

I sit back in my chair and smile. "Well please pass along to Mr. Radford I appreciate his suggestion, but we would just like the old one repaired. Is there anything else, Jacob?"

He nods, "Miss, I think you should look at the file for the woman Mr. Sterling gave you this morning."

"Et tu, Jacob," is all I say as I put my head on my desk.

"Miss, your actions *are* a bit dramatic. I know you have your reasons for not hiring women except when you feel it is absolutely the only option."

I pick my head up off my desk and lean back in my chair. "Jacob, my gut is telling me this smells bad. I try to weigh in all the factors when it comes to hiring, but this time I have to go with no".

Jacob considers this. "Is there not someplace you could asses her where perhaps your gut could be proved right or wrong?"

I narrow my eyes at my trusted Major Domo, "My gut tells me you are pushing this issue because you suspect something. Why not tell me what you're thinking?"

"Miss, I find some things can only be fully realized when they are exposed to the light." I hate when he gets all philosophical. It pisses me off.

"Fine, tell the chicken ass old man that the sun is shining on his ass today."

"Yes, Miss," he says as he leaves my office.

Jacob has something up his sleeve, but that will be a concern for later. What a fucking mess.

There's a heavy slow knock on the door and I know

it's Jack. I hit the button under my desk to open the doors. He comes in and silently makes his way to my desk.

"The demon said you wanted to see me."

"You know you should be nicer to him. He came in here to plead your case about the female."

Jack looks more than a little surprised. "Uh, believe me, *I* didn't ask him too. How did he even know?"

"The man *knows* everything. He has ears everywhere; you know that. He also may have a dog in this fight, but that remains to be seen. Jacob put forward the idea of putting her in a neutral environment to see if my gut is right or wrong. What do you think?" I cross my arms over my chest and lean back in my chair.

Jack isn't sure what to say. No doubt it has more to do with the fact he didn't think I would change my mind. "We could ask Veronica if we could use the island training ground. Take a few teams and see what happens."

I look at him before leaning forward and picking up a pencil to throw at him. "Make the phone calls. I'll choose the teams."

He stands up and places the pencil on my desk, "Today the dog is getting a sun burn on his ass."

I roll my eyes, shake my head and reach for the phone.

The connection takes a minute since it's a secure line. "Dungeon, how can I help you?" Lyle's Alabama drawl makes me smile.

"Lyle, I need a whole team. Do we have enough people in detention to declare their hotel reservation expired?"

"Yep," Lyle says. "Let me handle it darlin' and you'll be fartin' through silk."

I roll my eyes and chuckle. I have no idea what he means, but he's always full of southern down-home-isms.

"You jes' tell me when and where."

"Jack will be calling you with the final travel plans. We'll leave in about a week. Make sure all of those checking out are prepared."

I hang up and call Veronica. She doesn't answer so I leave the single word 'Dude' on her voicemail. I turn my seat towards the TV and start to watch the Six Nations match playing in the background. After a few minutes I move to one of the comfy chairs to continue watching the match. Jacob at some point dropped off some food. He has also left my office doors open.

I hear a knock and look up to find Cane standing in the doorway. As I chew on my sandwich I wave him in.

He comes over to the chairs and sits down. "Jack says we're going on a trip." It was as much a question as a statement.

I finish chewing, "Jack and his co-conspirator have come up with a way for the female to show her skill set in an environment I can control. In all fairness I've decided to send her and the other prospective recruits through the gauntlet and see how they do."

He gives me a strange look. "The gauntlet?"

"It's usually the final step in the initial application or promotion process. The exhibition you put on in the bar and Jack's gut were enough to get you hired without it. However, rest assured, you *will* eventually be sent through it." I hand him the bag of chips I've been snacking from.

Cane nods and takes a handful of Donna's home-made tortilla chips. He joins me in silence to watch the remainder of the match. When it's over Cane squeezes my shoulder as he walks by me.

I turn off the TV and go back to my flat. My phone is vibrating in my back pocket. I take it out and see its Veronica.

"Dude," is all I say.

"What's up, Dude?" is her response.

"Where are you?

"On the island, girl, making sure the sun goes up and down."

Veronica is a friend who is famous, or maybe more accurately infamous, and a bit crazy. Crazy, but not crazy, crazy, crazy; I couldn't do *that*. She leads a lot of lives. The life which matters to me right now is she likes to watch sweaty men run around and play commando. We have been friends since well before either of us knew where our lives were going. There were times she needed my help and I was there for her. And, there were times I needed her, and she never failed me.

She and I pooled some of our wealth into a nice little shell company. Veronica spends most of her free time on one of the islands our company owns. She also oversees the maintenance of the training facility. Of course, I think the real reason she does it is so she can watch the men train and perhaps steal some sweet stuff from the company man-candy-jar.

"We're looking at joining you in a few weeks. Are you going to be around? Also, so you know, this will be a house cleaning situation."

"Yeah, dude, I'll be here. I'm between movies right

now and the island is a stalker-free place. Hell, all I gotta do is hit one button and this place has no internet."

I laugh. "Sweet, I'll give you a call before we get on the planes. If you would please prepare my house as well as the big house it'd be greatly appreciated. Also, we'll need the usual place to store the cleaning supplies."

"No worries, dude, I'll make sure everything is taken care of."

I hang up the phone and go back to my room to lie down for a minute. I find myself nodding off, so I do the grown-up thing and change clothes before getting under the covers.

✷✷✷✷✷

The next day is spent making sure we have everything we need for the trip. Usually we have months to plan a trip like this. With the shortened time line, I want to make sure nothing is missed.

I send Jack a text asking him to join me for dinner. He shows up, but I can tell he's a bit confused as to why it's only the two of us.

I laugh to put him at ease. "No need to look all paranoid."

He keeps looking at me, still worried I can tell, but he takes a seat anyway. "Are we actually going to eat?"

"Yes, we are actually going to eat. Jacob will be here any minute with dinner. Now, whether it's poisoned is another story." I push his shoulder as I walk past him to take my seat.

Jacob appears like smoke, pushing a cart. I'm not sure what's under the silver lids but it smells amazing.

He puts the plates on the table, uncovers them and walks away without a word. Jack looks at me before taking one of the large spoons from the table to start to fill his plate. "Okay, so what's this about?"

I take my time putting food on my plate mostly because I know it will annoy him. After a good three or four minutes of messing with my food and taking a few bites, I set my fork down. "I think we should have Cane join us for a training session. Since he hasn't been sent through the gauntlet and he will not be joining this next bunch, I don't want the guys to think he's getting special treatment."

Jack has an overly full mouth of food. I'm really hoping he at least swallows some of it before he tries to answer me. He looks as if he's thinking but he might be concentrating on not choking. It takes him a few minutes to clear out his mouth enough to talk.

"I don't think it's a *bad* idea, but it's not like the others haven't seen the footage from the bar. My only concern would be we need to make sure not to hurt him too bad as we put him through the paces. He's not gonna want to sit out the island trip."

I take few more bites of food before continuing. "I've called Lyle and told him we'll need an entire team. This should almost clean out the detention level."

Jack only nods so I continue. "I've also spoken to Veronica and asked her to have the houses ready and the cells cleaned." Jack nods again. "Do you have anything to add to this conversation?" I ask him before throwing an olive from my salad onto his plate.

"First, Kenny isn't at one hundred percent, but he'll still be able to make the trip. It's a definite plus he's out of the stupid chair, but I think he should stay in the control tower. Second, Eric has put together the training teams. I know you said you would do it, but I spoke to him earlier and he has been thinking about an island trip for a while. I told him to run with it. Worse case we have to change up some of the details."

He pulls a piece a paper from his front pocket and pushes it towards me. I open it and find a short, nicely typed list with a rough layout of who will be where. Jack starts to talk again before I can ask any questions.

"The short of it is all the guys who will be part of the exercise on the ground are possible prospects for the teams. The guys up high in Over Watch are Eric's team and will be giving us the play by play from their positions. The prospective female employee will be sent out like all the rest. The guests from the cells will be let loose on the island with weapons and we will have to see what happens." Jack leans forward on the table.

I in turn lean back in my chair and think about everything he's said.

We finish eating in silence. Once Jacob has taken the plates away we spend the rest of the evening trying to work out what needs to happen between now and our departure. The goal is to accomplish an acceptable training session for Cane without breaking anything on any of the participants. I know Jack will keep most of it to himself because knowing everything can be harmful rather than helpful.

I make sure he understands the session needs to accomplish two things. First, we must show the others Cane isn't getting a pass on his training. This, of course, means he'll not only have to go hand to hand with Eric, but he'll need to face off with me as well. Second, we need to make sure not to do so much damage he ends up as a decoration on the island. Once Jack has finished scrawling out his notes he thanks me for dinner and lets himself out.

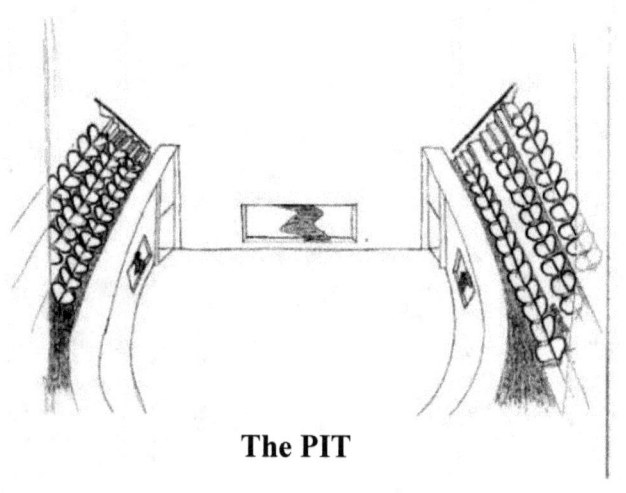

The PIT

SIXTEEN

The next week is used to review other potential candidates as well as putting in plenty of hours at the range. Kenny, Eric and Cane spend the days training. Jack, on the other hand, spends most of the week with the guys who recommended the female to him. Part of me thinks he's trying to convince himself this whole cluster-fuck is still a good idea.

When Sunday rolls around I text all four of them and tell them we have a dinner meeting at seven p.m. They arrive together, and we take our seats. Jacob and Drew bring in the food. They uncover the platters and leave us to our discussion.

I decide to start. "So, how many promotions will be on board for this trip?"

Eric takes a drink of his beer and tells me we have five who are up for promotions. He pulls a list of names from his back pocket and hands it to me. I read it over only because he's prepared it and brought it with him. I don't question any of the choices because I know Eric knows what he's doing.

I turn to Kenny, "Joker, you'll be joining us, but you'll have to remain in the tower. If you don't like the assignment, you can remain here."

Kenny smiles. "I'm happy not to be left behind. So, the tower sounds like a good time to me."

Jack picks this as the moment to talk to Cane. "Cane, we will be putting you through some training in the morning. It will be various scenarios involving Eric and others. None of the other guys would say anything, but you fast tracking from the garage to the penthouse without at least one trip through the gauntlet can't be setting well with some of them. So, we think it's important they see a real display from you before we leave. Fair warning, be prepared for anything."

Kenny is laughing quietly, and Eric is trying his best to get him to stop.

"Kenny, is there something you would like to share with the class?" I ask him.

He puts his hand up to ask for a second. He collects himself and asks, "Cane is going head-to-head with Eric and a bunch of crazies?"

In response I shrug my shoulders. "I don't know exactly *what's* going to happen. Jack set it up." I raise my eyebrow at him hoping I've answered his question.

Eric looks at Cane. "So, what do you think about this?"

Cane looks at Jack and then to me. "Well, I'm sure as hell not gonna be left here, so if squaring off with you and whoever else is the price I have to pay… Then I'll gladly pay it."

Jack can't help himself. He starts laughing and reaches across the table to shake Cane's hand. Eric and Cane tap their beer bottles together in lieu of a handshake.

We finish up our meal and chat about everything but the trip. Once they have all gone I spend some time zoning out in front of the TV. I get a text from Jack asking if I'm still in for training in the morning. I respond with simply, "go away."

He responds, "See you at 8."

I hear Jacob walk behind the couch and I'm assuming he's there to set out my clothes for the morning. It's not like I can't do it, but it seems easier to let him take care of it.

Thinking at eight o'clock in the morning is *not* something I do well. It's not long before I find myself nodding off, so I make the short walk to my bedroom. After throwing all my unneeded clothes on the floor I crawl into bed. It's not but minutes before I fall asleep.

***** *****

The alarm on my phone is beeping incessantly. If I didn't need the damn thing, I would chuck it against the wall. I slap at it until the beeping stops.

Time to begin the slow process to being human; I put in a new set of contacts, brush my teeth and find the clothes Jacob set out for me. I do my best to put them on right side out, but to be truthful I don't really care. If none of my female bits are hanging out, I consider it a win. By the time I'm done today, the damn things will smell as if I've had them on for a month, not to mention blood will be all over them. For Jack, a day of training without blood is a failed day of training.

I grab a hair tie on my way to the front door. I enter my code on the door locks and lean my head against the cold metal waiting for the click. When I finally hear it, I pull the heavy door open.

One of my security detail looks up from his computer, "Boss, Jack asked you to meet him in the training theatre."

I wave letting him know I heard him. At this time

of the morning it's considered a good response from me and the best he's going to get.

I take the elevator to the training level. I know I should take the stairs to warm up or whatever, but leaning on the elevator walls is currently more appealing. The doors open, and I turn towards the training room. I stop short when I remember I'm supposed to go to the theatre. I turn and make my way down the opposite hallway.

The training theatre is a Romanesque arena style room. It is one of Jack's bright ideas. The room sits about two hundred people. The viewing seats crawl up the sides of the walls to the fire exits. At the bottom of the seating area is a large space I call The Pit. We don't always use this room for this kind of spectacle. Usually it's used for training scenarios.

I see Kenny standing outside one of the doors. He whistles and jerks his head for me to follow him. He leads me into the observation space. From this room we can see the theatre is almost full. There are some empty seats toward the top, but not many.

Kenny hands me a note as the theater goes dark. It's in Jack's scrawl; it says, 'Don't forget to stretch'. I crumple it up and throw it back at him. I get his mischievous grin in response.

The space is dark for a few moments and then a solitary light over the pit the starts to glow. Cane is standing alone in the center. He doesn't look confused, simply alert.

Kenny turns to check if I have any reaction, but I know my face reveals nothing.

One of the side panels opens and Eric enters the pit.

Cane adjusts his posture to one of defense.

Jack's voice fills the room. "Gentlemen, this fight will be a last man standing situation."

Eric and Cane turn and face off. They circle each other slowly, looking for a weakness, a lapse in defense, any kind of an opening. It's supposed to be a training session, but both men realize there is a lot riding on the outcome. Eric wants to demonstrate his honed skills and Cane needs to prove he's more than capable of the responsibilities we have given him.

Cane is up first. He tries a leg sweep which Eric avoids. But Cane doesn't get his head out of the way fast enough and catches a swinging fist right under the eye. Eric can be a sneaky bastard when he fights.

Cane quickly shakes it off, but has started to bleed from the cut under his eye. He counters with a quick jab of his own, landing it just above Eric's right eye. The two continue to trade bone cracking strikes and kicks, neither getting close enough to take the other down. They seem to be working on finding the chink in the other's armor.

Cane manages to catch Eric with an elbow opening a gash between his upper lip and his nose. Not to be outdone Eric forces Cane to slip in the blood on the floor. This gives Eric the advantage he needs to get Cane in a ridiculous wrestling hold. Eric has Cane stretched out over his own body with Cane's arms and head trapped under Eric's left arm. Eric is relentless with the blows to Cane's exposed kidney's and rib cage. It's hard to tell if Cane is spitting up blood from internal damage or if he managed to get some in his mouth at some point.

I almost feel bad for Cane because I have no doubt Eric is using some of the residual grief he's carrying around from Patrick's death. Cane uses his flexibility to swing his knee up and catches Eric below the ear. This allows Cane to get in a rabbit punch of his own and roll away. It's not long until Eric has blood coming from his lip, nose and eye. No matter how much blood there is or how much it hurts, Eric will keep coming back for more. This could be painful for both of them, if it goes on for too long.

Not to be out done in the rage category, Cane is clearly fighting from whatever dark place keeps his internal fire burning. He's showing Eric no mercy despite being covered in a fair amount of blood which isn't his.

Eric gets a clean shot in and Cane's left eye begins to bleed. His face is half covered in a mask of blood.

I feel a nudge at my elbow and I look at Kenny. He has a black head bag and my KA-BAR Snake Charmer in his hand.

"Really?" I ask him, more annoyed than anything else.

He bends over to put the knife in my boot. He stands up and flashes his damn smile as he puts the bag over my head. Before I can say anything else I feel bodies moving around me and my hands are zip tied behind my back. Then in one quick movement I end up in the horrible predicament of being thrown over someone's shoulder like a sack of grain. I *hate* this position. It's hard to breathe, not to mention it makes you want to pee. I hear one of the panels to the pit open and I can see light coming through the bag. I get a simple tap on the hip before I'm lifted off whomever and lowered down to what I can only assume is the floor.

I feel the bag over my head loosen. Concurrently, I feel a sharp poke near my chin. The bag is removed but I leave my eyes closed. This is for two reasons. I need my eyes to adjust and I need to listen. Oddly the only thing I can hear is breathing. I slowly open my eyes and see Cane and Eric have now turned to face me and whoever is behind me.

Eric leans in and says something to Cane, who never takes his eyes off mine. He only nods at whatever Eric said.

Eric starts to circle towards my left and Cane goes the other direction. I'm not sure what these two have in mind, but this is probably not going to go the way they think it will. I almost feel bad for them.

I can see in my peripheral Cane is moving a bit quicker than Eric around the circle. Whoever has me takes this opportunity to extend his knife hand toward Eric. He moves his other hand from my zip tied hands to the back of my neck. In most cases this would be a bad plan, but his hand almost completely wraps around my neck. I can no longer see Eric, but I can see Cane is less than happy about the current situation.

The giant of a man has a hold of me and is using my body as a shield to fend off Cane. So far, it's working. I manage to reach down and lift the leg of my pants enough and Cane catches a glimpse of the knife in my boot. He doesn't look frustrated, simply annoyed. I can feel there's contact being made between this bear of a man and Eric. I can't really tell if anyone is winning, but Eric is managing to pull the big man's attention and grip away from me.

Cane sees his opening and takes it; he slides on his

knees behind me. He removes the Snake Charmer from my boot and cuts the zip ties on my hands. As I hit my knees he grabs me with his right arm, still knife in hand. He also takes a free shot at the back of the bear's knee with a hard-straight left.

The big man goes to one knee and Eric comes over the top and punches the big man square on the button. His giant saucer eyes glass over and he falls flat to the floor.

I pick this as my moment. I rush Eric going for his eyes. He quickly steps to the side, but not without giving me a small push. This knocks me off balance, but I maintain my footing. I can feel Eric coming up behind me and I step heavy on my front foot and mule kick him in the chest to get myself some space to work.

The kick has the desired effect. I circle around keeping my eyes on them. Cane isn't watching me; instead he has his eyes focused on Eric. I crouch down and pick up the knife the man-bear had in his hand. I lunge at Eric, but I don't get out of the way fast enough as he counters and catches me in the eye. My eyebrow is split open and I can feel the blood running down my face. I flip the knife in my hand and use the handle to catch Eric in the gut. He sucks in a deep breath and chokes a bit. I quickly sweep my leg around and take him off his feet. In my peripheral I can see Cane is making sure no one interferes.

Eric quickly gets to his feet and once again I don't get out of range fast enough. He slaps me hard enough to rattle my teeth. It knocks me to my knees and the knife from my hand.

"Exactly what you get for trying to play with the

big dogs," Eric growls. "You should've stayed under the porch."

I see Cane start to move towards him and I hold my hand out. I'm counting on this being enough to stop him. It halts his forward progress at least for the moment. I grin at Eric and spit a mouthful of blood at him. "I hate to say it, but you hit like a girl."

Eric steps back and thrusts his leg forward, foot aimed at my head. I roll under his extended leg and come up behind him. I turn quickly and punch him hard enough in the ass cheek to collapse his planted leg. He goes down in a howling heap to his knees. Cane takes this as his spot and punches Eric square in the jaw.

With blood still coming at a pretty good pace from my eye and my mouth I see Kenny and Jack have come into the room. Cane comes to stand next to me. I turn and push him with enough force he must regain his balance. "What the fuck is *this* shit? In case you have forgotten the terms, this was to be between you and Eric. Now it's between you and me." I slap him across the face. Cane doesn't look surprised or confused. It's a little disconcerting. I attempt to slap him again, but he grabs my wrist. He quickly tries to grab my neck with his free hand. I manage to block his attempt and he lets my other arm go.

I step back away from him, yet he advances. He takes a swing, but over rotates enough and I manage to get under it and take a shot at his kidney. This stuns him for a second, but he turns quickly and advances at me again. I check the floor and find Eric has managed to slide himself out of the way. I pick up my knife from the floor and this stops Cane but only for a second. He advances faster and walks right into the blade. A red stain appears on his chest. He takes advantage of my hesitation and sweeps my feet out from underneath me. Once again, I lose my weapon upon impact. All the breath in my lungs is gone as soon as I smack the floor. Before I can collect myself, he has his foot pressed firmly against my neck. This was his mistake. I reach up with both arms and twist his leg at the knee. I manage to pull him to the floor face down. I twist around to my side and give him a hard shot to the meaty part of his thigh before scrambling away from him.

Cane rolls over, but he doesn't move. He simply continues to sit on the ground.

I can tell he's working something out and I'm pretty sure I'm not going to like it. I see his hand move just in time. He picks up the knife, I left behind, and hurls it at me. It catches me on the edge of my shoulder. It stings like a bitch. I have less than a second to think about it before his body collides with mine. I barely get my elbow up, but I manage to catch him in the mouth with enough force, so he can't get a hold of me. I roll on top of him using my knees to squeeze the damage Eric was kind enough to inflict on his mid-section. Not to mention restricting his breathing. To further complicate things for him I'm fighting off his swinging arms as I'm throwing punches of my own.

Our blood is pooling together underneath his head. He jabs his thumb into the slice on my shoulder and I yell. Not in pain but in frustration. I use my other hand and all the power I have left to press on his carotid artery. He connects with my nose, which increases the blood loss. He's not holding back which was the point of this training session. However, this shit hurts. I see him start to fade, but the pain in my shoulder is almost strong enough to make me pass out. I lean forward to increase the pressure on his neck as well as his ribs. The pain in my shoulder begins to lessen and when I check to see why, I see Cane's hand is resting on my arm. I look down and he's out.

I collapse onto the floor next to him. I hear the guys in the seats pound their boots on the floor in respect. I yell, "Somebody get fucking medical in here!" I grin to myself and spit blood into the air in the process.

Kenny is the first to Cane's side and Jack stands over me. "Well there goes the beauty contest." Jack laughs.

The doctor and his staff fill the pit. Of course, Jack is not deterred by them. He squats down at my feet. I lift my head up to look at him. He continues with his colorful commentary. "Well if it wasn't for your last bit of effort, I was going to say he kicked your ass."

I laugh and wince. "Fuck you, you fucking fuck." I tell him as I lay my head back down.

"Don't move, Alex." I hear the doctor's voice over the commotion. Jack gets up and comes back with an icepack. He puts it under the back of my neck and puts his hand on my shoulder to keep me on the floor.

"Joker, tell me something." I yell because I can't see Cane or Eric.

I hear him laugh. "He says you hit harder than Eric."

Before I can answer I hear Eric's voice. "You can both go fuck yourselves." This causes most everyone standing in the pit to laugh.

The doctor gives his instructions to his staff. Cane

and I are to be stretchered down to the medical floor and Eric will be taken in a wheel chair. Kenny volunteers to push Eric while Jack walks to the elevators with the stretchers.

We are all sent through the x-ray process. Once the doctor determined we hadn't broken anything major he sent all three of us into the showers with temporary sutures. There are no fancy robes on the medical level just simple hospital gowns. When I walk back into the main room Eric and Cane are already there getting their various wounds looked after more thoroughly. I see Jack standing next to one of the private rooms. He jerks his head at the open door. I walk past both men without a word.

"Well, *that* was entertaining." Jack starts even before he has the door shut all the way.

I try to roll my eyes, but it hurts. "Shut up. What's the doctor say about those two?"

Jack sits down and puts his boots on the bed. "He says they need to be stitched up and soft foods until their jaws don't hurt. Also, Eric will need some massage therapy to help with the ass shot you gave him."

His last comment makes me laugh, but again, this is short lived because of the pain throughout my body. Jack points at my shoulder, "You're bleeding."

I flip him off. It's easier than getting up and beating on him. There's a knock on the door and without waiting for a response the doctor walks in. "Well I hope this little exercise served its purpose. Otherwise I may sedate all of you and put you in the cold room."

"Jack, I don't think the doc likes your training methods."

Before he can say anything, the doctor taps him on the head with his tablet. "Jack, get out." Rubbing his head Jack gets up and leaves the room.

The doctor inspects my face. He doesn't really say anything; he simply puts ointment on the cuts which don't need stitches. He then starts to sew up my eye. I can see he's annoyed. I sit still, mostly so he doesn't accidentally poke me in the eye out of sheer frustration. "Doc, you know being mad doesn't do any good. It had to be done."

He takes a deep breath and steps back to look at me. "Alex, I don't know why you put yourself through this. Those men could kill you and while they would be sad, it would be too damn late to do anything about it."

I take a beat before replying. I don't want the doc to think I'm not taking what he says seriously. "I understand and truly appreciate your concern. But this needed to be done. *I* need to know what these guys can do, how far they can go in a situation and *they* need to know it as well. I can honestly say I didn't expect it to get this bad, but I'm also not entirely surprised it did."

The doctor pauses for a moment and looks at the ceiling, as if thinking before he turns back to me. "Training," he smiles at me. "Their exercises are unbloody battles, and their battles bloody exercises."

I narrow my eyes. "What?"

"Flavius Josephus, a first century Jewish army captain and later historian. Of course your exercises are a bit bloodier. But, yes, the value of realistic training."

The doc seems to accept what I've said and gets back to work. He lowers the shoulder of my gown, so he can work on the damage Cane did with the knife throw.

"You're going to need to call your tattoo guy. The slice was already going to be significant and then when you add on the gouging Cane did the skin was separated even farther. I'll try to get the design back together as best I can, but I'm going to have to use staples to close it. I think your guy will need to make some repairs to the design."

I look over at the area he's working on. "Well, shit!"

The doctor finishes stapling and stitching all of us back together. He makes his best effort to hand out some low-grade pain killers. We all pass. We ride up in the elevator in silence and each go to our own quiet places for the rest of the night.

SEVENTEEN

Over the next few days everyone had their own things to occupy their time. There was still plenty to do before we left. Also, this helped to create the much-needed distance and focus we all required.

On the morning we are to leave for the island I find I still have some residual pain and stiffness from our little training session. This isn't going to stop me from going but it sure reminds me I *am* human. I open the door of the bathroom and I can smell the food Jacob has delivered. I can also hear voices coming from the main room. I guess this means we're all playing nice once again. I finish getting dressed and find the Four Horsemen all sitting along the island eating. Jacob has brought up pancakes, bacon, eggs and potatoes. I grab a plate and serve myself. Cane pours me a glass of red mystery juice and I make my way over to the big table.

Frankly it's still early and I'm not ready to talk to all of them yet, although, it's good to hear them chatting. I leave them to their breakfast and continue to eat mine while I read the articles Jacob has left me on the table.

Thirty minutes, five articles, and four pancakes later I can hear the guys scraping their plates into the trash and putting everything back on the tray Jacob left behind. Eric, Cane and Kenny leave the flat by way of the front door. Cane turns as he shuts the door and makes sure I see him, he nods and then lets the door shut after him. Jack sits down across from me and waits for me to say something as I silently return his look. He takes a deep breath and stands up. He stops before opening the door and turns, "You know we had to try it, right? The full combat thing with you, Cane and Eric? Gotta know how people will react." He nodded, "It's all gonna work out."

"Fuck off old man, just fuck off," is all I say to him in my calmest voice. I put my dishes with the rest and go to my room with the intent of packing, but instead fall back on the bed and stare at the ceiling. I hate packing.

I don't know how long I laid there before I hear the dishes clanking together. Shortly thereafter I hear Jacob's shoes clicking across the tile getting closer. The suitcases are open on the bed and I'm lying next to them. With nothing being said Jacob starts to pack my bags. I don't even try anymore. I have yet to travel anywhere and not have the clothes I need, so why fix it if it's not broken.

I hear a door close in the outer room. "Alex?" It's Cane.

"Bedroom," I yell at the ceiling.

I see him out of the corner of my eye as he steps into the doorway. "Hey, I wanted to check in with you before I headed down to the cars."

Jacob walks past him, taking my bags to leave them by the door. I hold my hand out and Cane helps me off the bed. We walk out to the living room without a word. Cane lifts his bag off the couch and slings it over his shoulder. He walks over and grabs the handle on my roller bag as he motions towards the door with his head. I let out a deep breath and pull on my messenger bag. I bump into him on purpose and open the door for him. We get on the elevator in silence and go down to the garage.

Jack is standing near the lead SUV and there are two large box trucks behind it, with Eric's SUV bringing up the rear.

I see Kenny is helping with the paperwork for the first box truck. This one is for the onsite applicants. These guys don't know what's about to happen or where they're going. They *do* know if they want a promotion they must complete this task. They know they could be hurt, but they also know dying is in no way part of the plan. You can train all you like, and simulators are helpful, however, until you are under live fire or you have someone coming at you with a machete and all you have is a rock, you never really know what you'll do.

Eric is overseeing the dungeon team. They are loading people from our onsite containment facility into the second box truck. These are people no one will miss and most of them volunteered to be our guest; some people will agree to anything to get out of prison. The female applicant and these guys will be brought to the island in a more roundabout way. Jack has decided with his buddies to bring the female to a different location to be collected.

The people in our containment facility are not promised anything other than an alternate place they can serve their time. However, at any given time they could be part of an experiment or training exercise. Again, they agree for the simple fact they get to leave prison. These same guests have bags over their heads. They're ankle and wrist shackled, all attached to their waist chains. Cane stops to watch them being herded to the truck.

"Is there something wrong?" I ask him.

"I was thinking how close I was to being with them instead of with you," he motions towards the lead SUV.

I think about what he said for a second and then kick him in the butt, "Open my door."

Once I'm seated Cane leans against the SUV waiting for all the work to conclude in case he's needed. I watch in the review mirror as Jack goes over the final paperwork with Kenny and Eric. Once all the equipment and people are loaded we pull out of the garage headed to the airport.

Upon our arrival there are two planes waiting for us. One is built for the transport of equipment and people who need chains. The seats in the front and the seats in the back are for our staff. They are comfortable, but not *too* comfortable. The seats in the middle of the plane each have slots under them. These are to secure the chains of our guests. Their seatbelt light never gets turned off.

The other one is the largest plane we own. Technically it can seat about a hundred people. We, however, have had it designed to comfortably carry about fifty people along with the luggage and any specialized technical equipment.

I watch as Eric and Jack oversee the loading of the inmates onto their plane. Kenny joins in with the rest of Eric's team as they start to board our plane. I stop Cane before he gets out of the SUV. "Grab me a spot next to the large table, please." He takes my roller bag to load it onto the plane with everyone else's and winks in reply.

I get out and watch as the transport plane's door closes and the SUV's pull away. Eric walks past me with

Jack close on his heels. When I turn around I find Cane standing at the top of the stairs with his arms crossed over his chest. I look up at the sky mostly to collect my thoughts. I take a few deep breaths and start for the stairs.

Once on board, I find Kenny stretched out on one of the couches towards the rear of the plane. He has a blanket and his tablet out. He already has a bag of hot gummy worms open and his headphones around his neck.

Cane is standing at my chair. He extends his hand out and I pass my messenger bag to him. I kneel next to Kenny. "Do you have everything you need?"

He gives me his damn smile. "Well, it's a bit cold and I *could* use someone to snuggle with."

I laugh and turn to Cane, "Can you get Joker a body pillow from the back? I'd hate for him to be cold."

With a bark of laughter Cane disappears to the back of the plane. He returns with a long body pillow and lays it down next to Kenny. "Here you go brother, feel free to name her or him whatever you like."

I start laughing again. Cane leans his leg towards my back for support, so I don't fall over, and I wrap my arm around his leg to steady myself. "Make sure you eat real food too, or no more gummies for you." I wink at Kenny as I un-wrap from Cane's leg before standing up.

The flight crew announces we are ready to depart. I stand up and grab water from the fridge. I look down the length of the plane and I can see things are as they should be. Some of the guys are eating and some are already starting to settle in to sleep. There's not a lot of talking. Jack and Eric make their way back to Cane and me. We wait to talk about anything until we reach a cruising altitude. The flight crew makes sure we have everything we need and then they make themselves scarce. Eric opens his portfolio and hands us each the assignments as well as an outline of the plan for the days to come.

There's not a lot of chatting; it's now all business. Cane asks Eric a few questions, but nothing unexpected. Eric and Jack leave the table to find their seats to get some sleep or at least to be alone.

Cane and I are left to ourselves and there is a moment of silence before he speaks. "I don't know why you're so mad at the old man and it's none of my business. However, for my own safety, can you tell me where it's safe to stand until this is over?"

I turn in my seat, so I can look directly at him. "The safest place for you to stand is the same place you have been standing since you first appeared in my flat. Just off my left shoulder."

He nods and stands. "I'm going to make sure Kenny is not violating his pillow and then I'm going to get some sleep. How long is the flight?"

I recline my seat into a lay flat bed and turn off the light. As I pull the blanket over myself I answer him. "You can probably get a full eight if you start now."

As he walks away I hear him say, "Smart ass."

* * * * *

I wake up mostly because I can feel someone looking at me. I open my eyes a fraction to find Kenny standing at the end of my makeshift bed. "Yes?"

He holds his hand up and shows me he's currently eating a carrot. "Old man told me to come and wake you. I decided to stand here was a better plan."

I clear my throat. "You have good instincts."

He nods and goes back to his couch.

I get up and stretch. Looking down the length of the plane I see everyone is up and getting themselves together. It's easy to tell the guys who are there to attempt the training grounds and those who have already been there. It's a look in their eyes and in how they carry themselves.

The flight crew lets us know we are making our final approach. Eric gets up and hands head bags to each of the guys who are applying for promotion. The men put the bags on and wait for further instruction. Our candidates will have to make it past the first obstacle which is a dead drop on an island, about an hour's swim to the training grounds.

Cane is helping Kenny with the paperwork. I don't see Jack, so he must be in the bathroom. I use the other one before the landing gear goes down. Not soon after I take my seat, we touch down on Veronica's island.

The men with the bags on their heads are led off the plane first. Eric and Jack move them from our plane to waiting helicopters. The rest of us unpack the gear into waiting oversized beach ready golf carts. We each grab a seat and our drivers take us to our respective accommodations. The first stop for the golf carts is in front of the large dorm style building.

"Where do you want me?" Cane asks as the guys begin to unload their gear.

"Your choice, you can stay with Eric and Kenny here in the dorm or you can stay with me," I tell him.

He remains in the cart with me and waves at Eric and Kenny as we pull away.

Cane looks around and asks, "Is the old man not staying with us?"

I point over my shoulder with my thumb. Cane turns to see Jack walking up to the main house.

"Jack stays with Veronica when we're here. It's not something we talk about."

Cane nods his understanding. This is another reason why Cane gets to skip the island for now; he knows when to talk and when to shut up. When we get to the guest house, I open the door and realize Cane isn't behind me. I turn to find he has his weapon out and at his side.

"Relax, there are no locks on the doors here. There's no need for them. The island is patrolled by armed guards and there are gun boats to keep the pirates away." He puts his weapon away, shakes his head and follows me into the house.

The house is pretty much a giant room with two levels. The bedroom is in a loft overlooking a large open living space. Cane is looking around for what I'm sure is another room.

"There's only one room." I point to the upstairs. Cane looks a bit more lost.

"The bed is gigantic, and you can sleep there, or you can sleep down here on one of the squishy couches. It's up to you. There's no Jacob here so as far as food goes we fend for ourselves." I grab my roller bag and start up the stairs.

"Well shit," is all Cane says as he follows me up the stairs. I start to unpack while Cane stands at the top of the stairs looking around the space.

"You weren't kidding; this bed is big enough for five guys my size!"

I laugh, "Don't judge me." It was Cane's turn to laugh.

He puts his clothes away and we go back downstairs to get something to eat.

"So, what exactly are we doing here?" Cane asks as he starts to make each of us a rather large sandwich.

"We are going to watch people be killed. Then we'll promote those who do it best." Cane had a mouth full of food and stopped chewing in what I think is probably contemplation.

"Not exactly what I was expecting to hear," he says over a mouth full of food. I look at him with a raised eyebrow.

Cane and I are finishing up our sandwiches when Jack walks up to the large sliding doors and lets himself in. "So… Eric says everything is ready and Marcus says he's ready to release the hounds from his location."

I drink some of Victoria's fancy bubble water and burp like a trucker. Jack shakes his head and eats the remaining chips from my plate.

"Marcus wants to do a night start?" I ask.

"Yeah," Jack laughs, "he knows how much you don't want to do this and he feels a night start will thin out the herd early. Given the temperature and wildlife it may very well take care of them all before they can even get to the training grounds."

I nod. "Marcus has a point. I'm *not* looking forward to the end game with all of this. I know you have high expectations, but I don't see it working out."

Jack gives me his evil eye. "*You*, are truly a regular ray of sunshine."

I can tell Cane is trying to figure out what's going

on without having to ask any questions. He's not going to intervene because he knows it could get him excluded, so he picks up the plates and puts them in the sink.

I slide off my stool. "I'm going to take a nap. What time do we need to be at the boats?"

Jack looks at his watch and looks out the giant glass doors. "I think we need to be to the island before sundown. Let's meet at the boats at seven o'clock."

I give him two thumbs up and start up the stairs. "Cane you can either nap up here or down on the couches. Either way, you need to sleep. Trust me when I tell you whatever sleep you got on the plane will not be sufficient for the night's activities."

"See you at the boats old man," Cane says as he slaps Jack on the back and starts up the stairs after me. I hear the front door shut without a word from Jack.

Cane grabs some clothes, goes into the bathroom and shuts the door.

The quilts at the foot of the bed are meant for naps so I am glad Veronica got them out for me. I hear the water in the shower turn on. I put a king size quilt on the one side of the bed for Cane and I keep the shirtless cowboys one for myself. I take off my shoes and get comfortable. The water turns off and after a few minutes I hear the door open.

"Do you want me to turn the TV on?" Cane asks.

I wave my hand at him. "No, there are no sounds to drown out here. The quiet is nice sometimes."

He laughs quietly as he looks at my quilt. "So, you get shirtless cowboys and I get... What...? Geometric shapes?"

"I *would* give you the cowboys, but I am already comfortable."

He laughs again, and I barely feel the bed move under his weight.

The size of the bed is no joke. It was custom made and at least two King size beds wide and one and half King size beds long. It's good for reenacting the days of Caligula…or naps.

"Damn!" Cane says. "I thought all the pillows at your flat were Jacob's doing. *You,* however, seem to be the one with the pillow addiction."

I laugh and toss a pillow in his general direction.

"Careful, you almost made it all the way over here."

I double check my phone to make sure the alarm is set and then quiet fills the room.

✳✳✳✳✳

My brain is trying to remember where I am and where the alarm sound is coming from. As the fog in my head begins to clear I know there's someone else in the bed and they are close, much closer than they should be. I open my eyes and I can see Cane sitting up with his eyes closed. I'm assuming he's asleep.

I feel a warm spot on my shoulder. I follow the line of his arm and he has one hand on my shoulder. This is all a bit disconcerting, yet I don't say anything; I simply roll over towards the side of the bed where I started and turn off the alarm. I stretch, get up and gather my change of clothes to take my turn in the bathroom.

Forty-five minutes later I emerge dressed and alone on the second floor. As I come down the stairs I find

Cane and Jack having coffee. My tea is waiting for me on the counter. I thank Cane for the making it for me.

"How do you know I didn't make your tea for you?" Jack says, rather annoyed.

"You don't even make your own food. *Why* would I assume you made my tea?" I push him almost hard enough to knock him off his chair. "Anyway, I thought we were meeting at the boats?"

"Well," Jack chuckles, "I had to make sure you hadn't chained him to the bed and if you *did* I wanted to get here in time to get some good photos."

Cane laughs, I simply roll my eyes.

Jack's satellite phone rings and he motions towards the door.

"Cane, if you would be so kind as to grab the weapons out of the closet please."

He sets his coffee down. "Sure, which one?"

I motion to a door near the staircase. He walks over and opens the door; he unzips the bag and whistles. He zips it closed and hefts the bag onto his shoulder.

"Okay, let's get this over with," is all I say as I follow Jack out the door.

When we get down to the boats, Kenny and Eric are already waiting for us. Along with them are Eric's team leaders. Everyone nods at each other and we get in.

We make the trip to the training grounds in silence. At about the thirty-minute mark the island comes into view. The men piloting the boats know where we're going so there's no need to communicate. As we pull up to the docks, the remaining members of Eric's teams, in full combat gear, are waiting for us. They look like they're about to bring down a warlord rather than simply participating in an employee screening exercise. When the last of the gear is unloaded from the boats, the drivers wave and depart. I take a minute to watch them grow smaller on the horizon.

I turn and look at the men standing before me, making eye contact with Eric, Kenny, Jack and Cane before I address the group. "All of you know how this goes. We have people who want to make the teams. They will be going head to head with a team of convicts, lifers. If the good guys need saving then you save them, do not shoot unless it will save their life. If any of the lifers decide they want off the island they are to be taken down. If any of the applicants decide they don't want to be in our employment anymore, Jack or I will make the call as to what will be done with them. If any of them for any reason turn on their fellow applicants, they are to be put down immediately, any questions?"

Everyone nods understanding the rules of engagement. Eric lifts his finger and moves it in a circle, the silent signal for everyone to disperse. They all disappear quietly to their assignments.

I watch their backs as they scatter and then begin my walk towards the watch tower with Kenny next to me. Cane follows as Jack brings up the rear. The sun is about to set as we make our way into the very sterile tech facility. There are multiple screens and they are currently showing images from cameras all over the training area. We also have cameras on the weapon scopes as well as body cameras on all the participants. Eric's men in the over-watch positions also have cameras.

Cane stands at the back of the large room, quietly taking in his environment.

Jack's tech guys are making sure the sound and visuals are all ready to go. They give him a thumbs up and Jack checks in with Eric to make sure his men are ready.

"Joker," I tap Kenny on the shoulder, "unless this building is on fire you stay in here. Do you understand what I'm telling you? You are still not field ready, and I don't want anything causing a setback in your recovery."

Kenny takes a seat at the giant console and checks in with the snipers. He turns in his chair to look at me with his unique grin. "Yes, Ma'am," is his smart-ass answer as he winks at me.

I shake my head and push a call button on the control panel. "Lyle, are we ready?"

I notice Jack takes this moment to call the drop island to tell them we're ready.

There's a moment of silence and then I hear his Alabama drawl. "Yep, the bait is ready. Good huntin'."

Jack motions toward the monitors and I can see the signals from the other island have been lit. This lets us know the applicants have entered the water.

A group of Jack's men are in boats. They're there to make sure anyone who dies on the swim ends up at the bottom of the ocean. If a candidate gives up during this part, they are removed from the water, sedated and taken to another island for evaluation. The men in the boats are in constant communication with Jack which works for me.

We monitor the candidates as they make their way across the water. Of the fifteen people who start the swim, thirteen make it to shore.

I hit the call button. "Lyle, open the cages."

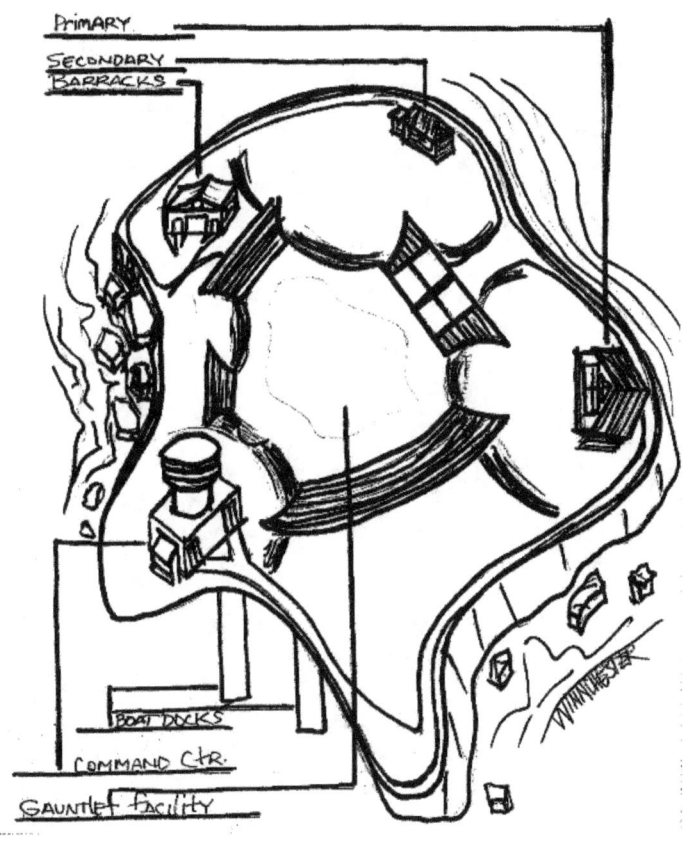

Primary

Secondary
Barracks

Boat Docks

Command Ctr.

Gauntlet Facility

WINCHESTER

The TRAINING ISLAND

EIGHTEEN

An alarm sounds over the island. This lets us know the thirty lifers have been let loose on the training grounds. Outside the cages are several tables. They hold every kind of hand-held weapon a person can think of. Our guests were told they can take as many or as few as they like. They were also told ammunition as well as other weapons can be found all over the paddock. Their goal? Stay alive. It makes for better competition for the employees if the other guy thinks he might gain his freedom if he survives. Truth is the inmates will never see another sunrise.

Now, we don't broadcast this little event and we don't take bets, not even among ourselves. This is justice in its purist form; all our guests have committed heinous crimes against humanity. This little exercise also helps Jack and I find the right kind of people. As the applicants come ashore there are packs with numbers they were assigned before they left the drop zone. They were told about the weapons on the island and were instructed about the obstacles they must overcome. We watch as the applicants put on their dry clothes left in the numbered packs. They check their weapons and make their way through the large gates.

On some of the other monitors we can see the lifers are starting to take up positions to perhaps partake in their own one-person ambush style attacks. I continue to stare at the monitors with Jack next to me and Cane still standing back observing the controlled chaos.

It doesn't take long before the groups clash. A couple of the lifers are taken out quickly by one of the applicants. Jack appears to be impressed, but I don't think this guy can back his fitness. He's all fire and then steam, but time will tell.

Cane moves closer to us as more contact is made between the two factions.

I lean over and whisper in Kenny's ear. "Joker, find the female and put her on the top center monitor."

He laughs and rubs his ear. It doesn't take long for him to find her and get her up on the screen. She appears to still be rather close to the gates. This bothers me. For some reason my gut turns over. My instincts are telling me this isn't right. Something is going on.

Cane makes short work of the space remaining between us. He's now standing directly behind my right shoulder.

"Cane," I whisper over my shoulder, "if you'd please get my weapon out of the bag."

Cane doesn't say a word; he simply goes back to where he put the bag down and brings it back to the monitor station. He places it on an empty chair and opens it, pulling out my HK 45, and the leg holster. I put on the weapon after making sure it's ready to go.

Cane removes a sheath from the bag as well with a large bowie knife in it. He pulls the knife to check the blade and hands it to me. I take it from him because I can also see it as a potentially good choice. It gives me a stealth option a gun would not provide me.

Jack reaches out in a half-hearted attempt to stop

me. I give him a hard look and he removes his arm from my path without a single word being spoken.

I'm out the door, down the stairs and onto the grounds before anyone can follow me. I can hear Jack in my earwig telling the guys in over watch I have entered the grounds. This is the only thing to give me a blink of pause. I know my actions have made their job more difficult.

I hear Eric tell the second half of his team to herd the party away from the gates. This is because it's the direction I'm headed. I hear Cane's voice in my earwig. This tells me Jack's convinced him to stay in the tower, but in a compromise, he gave him access to some of the audio controls.

"She's still near the gates." Cane tells me with what sounds like tension and perhaps a little confusion in his voice.

"Alex, do you care to share with the class what you're up to?" Jack asks, although I'm not sure he really wants an answer.

I flip off the nearest camera and hear Kenny laughing in my ear. I take cover behind a large tree. From here I can see my target crouched near the gates. She's rather well hidden behind a boulder. She would be hard to spot, if I didn't have my eyes in the sky.

I tap my throat mic, "Close the fucking gates." Nothing is said in response but in less than a second, I can hear the gates start to slide shut.

The two very large, independent gates slide from opposite directions and overlap in the center. I watch her as the gates begin to cross in the middle. She looks a bit panicked and I'm now convinced there is more going on here than any of us realized.

I can feel my anger starting to boil. "Get me Eric," I say into the mic.

In less than a second, I hear, "Boss?"

"Tell your boys near the gate they are not to fire on her. I will take care of this. Am I clear?"

I hear the radio clicks of confirmation from the team members in my ear. I take the time for a couple of deep breaths to focus.

"You're clear," is Eric's response.

I know Jack is furious and Cane has to be annoyed. I hear Cane's voice, "There is a single lifer headed toward the gate away from the main pack. He seems to be looking for something." There's a pause and then I hear his voice again, "Or maybe someone, damn it, Alex!"

"Kenny, I want to hear what they say to each other, and Eric, once they're done chatting, I want a hole in his head."

There's a second of dead air. Then Eric and Kenny reply in unison, "Affirmative."

I don't hear anything from Jack. I imagine he's trying not to shoot himself in the eye. However, Jack's melodramatics aside I know every instruction I gave will be followed without question. The lifer reaches the rock and our prospective female candidate. They embrace and kiss. It was not what I would have bet was going on, but at least my instincts were right. It's all very disgusting and beyond infuriating. I don't know who this lifer is, and I don't care. I'm more pissed *she* weaseled herself on to our island and the bitch believes she's going to get away with this.

I hear a crackle over the earwig. The conversation between the two idiots begins to fill my ear:

Male voice, "They closed the gate, how are we getting out of here?"

Female voice, "Don't worry, I have a plan."

Male Voice, "We're on a fucking island and I only know this because I heard one of the guys talking about it before we got on the plane. So even if we get out the gates, how do we get away?"

Female Voice, "If I must kill every one of those rent-a-thugs, we *will* get out of here. I know I heard boats on the water when I swam here from where ever."

Male Voice, "There are snipers. We can't out run'em all."

Female voice, "No one knows what's going on. I don't care what they say about her and her merry band of man-whores. She's not smarter than I am."

Male voice, "I'm starting to think your priority is not saving me."

Female voice, "Don't be ridiculous of course I came here for you, baby. *Everything* I've done is for you. Getting to kill her, Miss rich bitch, is a bonus."

I've heard more than enough of *this* soap opera. I'm watching the fool poke his head up like a damn ground hog every few seconds. I roll my eyes and I point to the center of my head and then I point in their general direction. I know the guys can see me. I hear the report from the weapon before I see the pink cloud.

She stands and screams at the sky, "You fucking bitch!"

I suspect she's yelling at *me*. I'm going to shake Jack until his teeth fall out for making me do this.

"You had *no right* to lock him away like an animal. You had *no right* to take him away from me. He didn't do *anything* wrong!" Her yelling is now mixed with snotty sobbing; it's all very daytime drama-esque.

Cane's voice comes over my earpiece. He informs me her beloved was a two-time loser and he was going to use his family money to get away with the rape of a woman he paid for sex. He also tells me the crime took place one county over. This simple sentence tells me a lot. The smaller counties around the state don't always have the resources or the manpower to pursue some of these cases. Not to mention the amount of influence some people can have in a small town can make law enforcement's job harder, especially for the honest ones. I move around the tree and stand in plain view, my hands in my pockets. She seems shocked to see me and at the same time I can see the hate boiling in her eyes.

"Do you know why he was locked up?" I can see her mind working. She's not thinking about the question. She's trying to decide how she wants to kill me.

"He was being railroaded; the girl was a hooker and liar," she yells at me.

"Was?" I note the interesting choice of words.

I hear Jack, "They found a female body in the desert. No hands and no head." I nod slightly letting him know I heard him.

There's the sound of screams and gunfire in the distance. She turns toward the noise, but quickly turns back to me.

She starts yelling again. "We were going to run

away together. With my training and his money, no one would have ever found us. You and your circus of misfits had to stick your noses where they didn't belong."

If I'm honest, she's boring me. I take my hands out of my pockets and begin to walk towards her. She picks up the backpack and dumps it out on the ground. She's quickly looking up and down, as I stop about 20 feet from her.

"I know this is some kind of perverted sex cult," she screams at me. "You brainwash these men and drug them and make them do unspeakable things! You tried to take him from me, but he loves me, and he turned *you* down. So, you locked him away. But I found you and now I'm going to make you suffer," she screams, waving her hands.

I shake my head in disbelief. "Wait a hot fucking minute. The guys I work with would not cut the hands and head off a woman. Also, not to harp on the obvious, but I think you mean he *loved* you. Past tense. He was a piece of shit and now the coward at your feet is fucking dead. Also, not to put too fine a point on it, but if this *was* a sex cult, I would be too damn exhausted to come out here and deal with your ridiculous ass."

She picks up the KA-BAR knife out of the dirt. I don't want to have to shoot her but having a knife fight seems like a waste of energy.

"How did you ever make it past the psych evaluation?" is all I can think to say to her.

"Oh, they tested me. They said I was *just crazy enough.*"

I shake my head, "Who is *they* exactly, the voices in your head or the animals who trained you?"

Her rage boils over. She makes her way quickly around the boulder and lunges at me. I step to the right and go down to a crouch. I pick up a two-inch-thick tree branch from the ground.

"I'm going to cut you open in front of all your little trained house boys," she growls. "I'm going to show everyone you're just another lying hooker who manipulates men."

As she turns to face me, I stand in one motion and throw a small stone. It nails her below the right eye. The impact surprises her and as she pauses for a split second. I swing the branch and catch her smack in the ribs. The distinct sound of bones breaking fills the air and she crumples to the ground. She makes a futile attempt to stab at me as I move closer to her.

"I want you to know up until a few minutes ago, I had no idea your hole-in-the head boyfriend was on this island. However, I'm not sorry he was here and I sure as hell am not sad he's dead."

She swipes at me again and misses. I swing the tree branch almost like a golf club and catch her below the elbow on her knife wielding arm. The sound of bone breaking has the same effect on the nervous system as nails on a chalkboard. She still has plenty of hate and fight, but her body is quickly becoming useless to her.

"You're a fool, people know I'm here. I have a tracker and there will be people coming for me." She spits blood on my boot for good measure.

I lean on the tree branch like a walking stick. "Think for a minute. Do you have a blank spot in your memory? A spot where you feel there should be something, but you're not sure if something is really missing."

I watch for her reaction. I see a slight squint of acknowledgement around her eyes. "Yeah, right there. You were scanned, poked and prodded before you ever got here. They found your little chip and took it out. If there are, in fact, people tracking you they will be looking for you on the rim of an active volcano a very long way away from here." I could see the defeat wash over her.

I can almost feel through the earpiece Jack's twitching around in the control booth. I know he thinks I'm dragging this out and he would be right. She's crying and spitting at me. I remove my gun from the holster and I turn it around in my hand. I smack her in the jaw with the butt of the heavy weapon. She can no longer spit blood but some teeth kind of dribble out of her mouth. I put my gun back in the holster and I squat down in front her.

"How dare you come to this island and try to hurt these men. How dare you presume your love for a raping piece of shit is more important than the work these men do. The mere fact you thought you could kill me boggles my mind. It was never going to happen because all of your training was based on delusions and lies!"

She looks me in the eyes. She uses her last bit of strength to push herself up onto her one good elbow. She reaches out for my leg to pull herself up a bit more. I let her because I can see her spirit is finally broken. I grab her by her blood matted hair.

I remove the knife from my hip and take the time to push my hair behind my ear. "Rugby, much like this island, has rules you have to follow. These rules help to keep order and respect in the utter chaos. They are known as the *laws of the game*."

I lean down and make sure she's looking right at

me. "I know you have more you would like to say to me, but I don't care." I drive the long bowie knife up behind her chin at an angle. I push it up into her skull and turn it once for good measure. As her body falls backwards to the ground she slides off my knife.

In my ear I hear Cane's calm voice. "Don't move."

I close my eyes and I hear a spit from a rifle and then I hear a body fall not far behind me. I open my eyes and turn to look over my shoulder. I see our smelly mountain man lying on the ground with a machete in his outstretched hand. Clearly, he had ceased to be useful. I stand and bow, making the gesture of doffing my cap in appreciation to the man who took the shot.

I touch the throat mic, "Jack, what's the count?"

"We have four who can move up. The rest are injured and will need to be evaluated. The last lifer was the one with the machete, Cane took care of him."

I nod and put my hands on my hips. "Okay get this cleaned up. Eric, if you would please take care of the four and get me updates on the injuries." I hear confirmation from both Jack and Eric.

I walk over and stand in front of the gates. "Joker, open the gates." I wait for them to open and walk down to the water.

I leave my weapons, electronics, and excess clothing on the beach. The ocean looks like black marble and the only light is the flicker from nearby torches. None of this discourages me from going into the water. I walk in up to my shoulders. It's cold, but not so bad I want to get out. Rugby players often talk about how much cold-water rehab is beneficial after a physical match. I'm starting to think they're right. I tread water for a few minutes and then dive down and stay under for a few seconds in the silence. I come up for air and look at the island.

I can see inside the cleansing fire has been started. I dunk my head under the water again and swim to the shore. I notice Cane standing next to my gear. He doesn't say anything; he simply hands me the towel he had over his shoulder. I dry my hair a bit and wrap myself in the towel. I sit down on my clothes, but he still doesn't say anything. He sits down next to me and looks out at the ocean.

I can hear muffled voices. I realize they're coming from the radio in his back pocket. He lets out a deep breath and yanks out the radio.

"Calm down old man," he says, "I'm with her. She decided to be eaten by sharks was a better prospect than talking to you."

Jack's response is a string of vulgar words. Cane puts the radio back in his pocket.

I can see Cane smile in the torch light. "You know I think I saw a cake in the fridge back at the house. It said happy birthday and had big orange flowers on each corner."

I stand up, stretch and look down at him. "Birthday cake should be its own food group."

He hands me my stuff and I drag my aching joints back to a waiting boat to return us to the island. I know things in the training ground are going to be put in order and most of it will be done by Jack personally. It will be his self-inflicted punishment for causing this huge cluster fuck. I'm not going to stop him. I find, in most cases people are harder on themselves if they are truly sorry for what they've done to cause others pain.

When Cane and I get back to the house I head straight up the stairs to shower. I get cleaned up and come back down.

Cane has left the house dark except for the candle lit lanterns inside and the torches outside the giant glass doors. He has also turned on the TV, finding, a Super Rugby game on the DVR. On the coffee table he has two large bottles of Pellegrino, a six pack of beer, the birthday cake, and a few bags of tortilla chips you can *only* find in one place in Las Vegas. I'm not sure how those got here, but someone is getting a raise or a hooker or both.

He must have used the outside shower because he has changed and no longer smells like gun powder or death. No words are said; he simply hands me a fork and pushes play on the remote. Any girl who says she only wants flowers, fancy food, and artsy films is crazy.

* * * * *

The sun shining on my face wakes me up. I look around and see the TV is still on, but the match is different from the one last night. I look over at the coffee table and I see the cake is gone. I'm assuming it got put away at some point during the night. I notice I'm covered with a quilt and I can see Cane is asleep not too far away from me on the couch. He has one hand resting on his weapon and the other one on my quilt. Even in sleep he seems very alert.

I stretch and run my tongue over my teeth. I would like to say I will never eat birthday cake again but hell; it would be ridiculous and a lie. I wrap the quilt around myself and go up the stairs. I quietly put in about an hour on the yoga mat before getting in the shower. When I emerge there's the smell of coffee and breakfast coming from downstairs.

I yell, "Head's up," before throwing my bag from the loft down to the living room.

I descend the stairs and find only Cane standing at the island stove finishing up a heart attack disguised as breakfast. The large glass doors are open slightly and a nice clean breeze is circulating through the room. I take a seat at the island and pour myself some orange juice.

Cane motions towards the large platter of bacon and sourdough toast. At this rate I will have to give Cane a raise because I will gain a million pounds and need additional security. Cane finishes up the egg and cheese omelets, slides them on to plates and pushes one in front of me.

He takes the seat next to me without a word. We look out at the ocean and eat in peace. When we finish stuffing our faces I take my jug of water out onto the patio. Cane puts the dishes in the sink and then puts ours bags next to the door.

He does a double check through the house to make sure we have everything. When he comes out to the patio he stands behind me, just off my left shoulder. He still doesn't say a word, but he rests his hand on my shoulder. I don't know how long we stayed standing there, but it was very peaceful.

The silence is broken by a knock on the front door. The knocking itself is odd since there are no strangers on the island. Cane squeezes my shoulder and goes to answer the door.

I turn and watch him walk to the door. His hand is resting on his weapon, clearly the knock seems odd to him as well.

He opens the door to find Jack standing there. "Why the fuck are you knocking?" Cane asks as he opens the door wide for Jack to come in.

Jack puts out his cigarette and makes his way into the house. "Is she pissed?" I hear Jack ask.

"Not with *me,*" Cane says, "but hell, we haven't said anything to each other since we got back here last night."

Jack nods and I can hear his boots moving closer to me on the patio. "Alex," is all he says as he takes a seat across from me. Cane resumes his position behind me.

I use my best professional voice. "Has everything been taken care of?"

Jack relaxes, but only slightly. "Yeah, the training grounds are as we found them, and all the debris has been disposed of."

I nod. "When can we leave?"

Jack leans forward with his forearms on his thighs. "Everything is ready; you give the word and we're out of here." He exhales rather loudly.

"Let's get back to civilization. We have clients to see and work to do." I don't say anything else. I stand and walk back through the house and out the door.

I hear Cane tell Jack, "Well at least she didn't shoot you, or, you know, kick you in the balls." Cane picks up the bags next to the door and follows me. Jack closes the door and joins us without another word.

*****

At the airstrip Eric and Kenny are overseeing the loading of the transport plane. Our four newly promoted are helping to load the injured onto the plane as well.

Kenny sees me, waves and I wave back. I turn back to the other plane. Jack and Cane are loading the gear and the bags. I wait for Eric and Kenny to finish up. Eric stops to speak with the newly promoted and lets them know they will be riding with us on the other plane. They pick up their bags and walk past me, each nodding before putting their bags with the others.

Eric is waiting for them at the top of the stairs to give them some basic rules and to tell them where they can and can't sit. Kenny comes over and stands next to me. "I don't know if it matters," Kenny says, "but the old man was a mess when we all finally saw what you had already picked up on. At one point he told Cane if something happened to you, he had his permission to shoot him. Cane was quick to let him know, if something happens to you, he would cut off his head."

I nudge his shoulder with mine. "It sounds like the soap opera I was listening to with the damn banshee. I do, however, find it interesting *you* were not going to avenge my death."

He turns to me and pulls his sun glasses down his nose and flashes me the full joker smile. "First, I knew there was no way the chick was going to take you out. Second, I told them both they should feel free to kill each other because it meant I would finally be able to make out with you in peace."

I shake my head and start to laugh. I reach up and push his glasses back up his nose. "Joker, I don't think I will ever be ready for *your* carnival ride."

He reaches out and squeezes my hand before he turns to start up the stairs. I can barely hear him telling the guys on the plane there better not be any newbies sitting on his couch. I laugh again and put my hands in my pockets.

I watch Jack and Cane board the plane and I take one last look around thinking about how soon I could be on the *other island*. The only problem being I know *he* isn't there. I run my hands through my hair and focus my thoughts.

I board the plane and take up a place on one of the couches. I've made the decision I'm going to sleep all the way back home. There's not a lot of talking on the flight back. Everyone keeps to themselves. I wake up and eat at one point, but it's not long until I'm back on my couch asleep.

*****

Upon landing in Las Vegas, we are met by three of the company SUV's as well as a medical transport. Jack, Eric and Kenny ride together to get an update on what's been going on in our absence. Cane and I get into my vehicle with my driver and we ride in quiet back to the offices. We pull into the garage and everything seems to be running smoothly.

I slide out of the truck and go directly to the elevator with Cane not far behind me. I can tell there's tension as we walk through the garage. I'm sure it has everything to do with word getting back about Jack ending up in the dog house. When he and I are not on the same page, it can cause the others to be unsure whose side to take.

As we exit the elevator on my floor the guards stand up as if at attention. I nod at them and the one to my right nods back. He reaches for the button under his desk to unlock the doors. Cane follows me in, shuts the doors and leaves my bag by the door. He looks at me as if he wants to say something but changes his mind. He nods and takes the back stairs to his own flat without saying a single word. I go into the bedroom, kick off my shoes and crawl into bed and immediately go back to sleep.

I wake up once again to the smell of food. When I open the door to look out into the kitchen, I see Cane cooking again. I'm not sure how I feel about this. On the island is one thing. Here in my flat is another story. I see Jacob moving around as well. This makes the entire situation even odder. I shut the door and decide a shower is the best course of action.

As I exit the bathroom I find clothes have been set out for me. Jacob strikes again.

I think he feels the events on the island were enough to make it necessary to have my clothes chosen for me. If nothing else it's helpful; it means I have less to think about. I finish with my lotion and hair routine. After putting on my clothes I count to seven before opening the door.

"So, why is Cane cooking in my kitchen?" I ask the room.

"Miss, the kitchen is preparing for a large party." Jacob gives a perfect nod of his head. "Cooking your breakfast here is much easier and Mr. Cane was nice enough to assist me."

I raise my eyebrow at him as I take a seat on one of the barstools.

"Good morning, boss," Cane's voice is flat.

"Where's Jack?"

"Miss, I believe he's on the training level." Jacob answers.

Cane smiles, "I think he's still punishing himself."

I shrug my shoulders. The old man can do whatever he wants at this point. My current priority is to get to my office. I need to make sure our business hasn't gone to hell while we were entertaining Jack's abysmal new female recruit idea.

"So, is the smaller cooking space restricting the breakfast to only bacon?"

Cane laughs and turns to push the buttons on the microwave. He opens the oven and removes a platter of pancakes, blueberry no less. The microwave dings and I watch him remove the syrup. If I was in the market for a new Jacob I might have to give the job to Cane.

"It's nice to see you have multiple job skills."

He only shakes his head and pours my orange juice.

EPILOGUE

4 months later...

I'm awakened by someone yelling my name. I'm still mostly asleep but I know it's Jack. I hit the light on the bed side table and Jack forces his way through the doors. "What the hell, Jack?"

He's grabbing random clothes from the closet and throwing them at me. "Get up; we've got to get to your island."

I don't question him; I make quick work of getting my clothes on. I dart into the bathroom to put my contacts in. "Jack?" I yell.

He appears in the doorway. "The emergency alarms were triggered, and we can't get any of the men on their radios. According to Eric you told him the island was being used."

I look at him and finally realize exactly what he's saying, and I know it's showing on my face. I pull on my boots, grab my phone and check for messages. There are none and the zero on the screen sinks in my gut like a boulder. I run through the living room and grab my bag off the couch in route to the elevators. I can hear Jack's boots right behind me. I also know he's on the phone confirming our plane is ready to go.

I hit speed dial on my phone and call the only person I know who can help us. "Tiny, it's me; get to the island as fast as you can. Take as many men as you can find; I'll pay whatever it takes. The alarms have gone off and he's there alone. Find him, Tiny."

I hang up and kick the elevator wall hard enough to leave a dent. I bend over at the waist trying not to throw up or scream as I close my eyes.

"Alex, what is he doing there alone?" Jack's question knocks the air right out of me.

The END

From Book 2

CYNICAL PLAY

"He was rehabbing an injury and contemplating retirement." I say to my reflection in the polished steel of the elevator.

Jack keeps pushing the button on the panel as if it will make it move faster. I know he just needs to do something. The doors open and my SUV is already running. I close the gap quickly, throw in my bag, pull myself into the seat and slam the door. Jack gets in and the driver puts the SUV in gear. He leaves a layer of rubber on the garage floor.

It's three in the morning so traffic to the executive airport is thin and my driver is not bothering to abide by too many traffic laws. I feel a hand on my shoulder and I whip around in my seat to find Cane sitting behind me in his usual spot. I look over at Jack and if looks could kill, Jack would have been vaporized.

"Cane, what the fuck are you doing? You're not needed on this trip. You can go back with the SUV".

"Jack thought you might need someone with my skill set. If you want me to stay here, I will," Cane says calmly.

We pull up to the airport and the workers open the gates without delay. The plane is ready and my driver unlocks the SUV doors while we are still moving.

I speak without turning around, "Something has gone horribly wrong and Jack is right; your skill set may in fact in be very useful. Get on the plane," I say to Cane as I jump out of the SUV.

I take the stairs in as few steps as possible and I nod at the pilot. I find my seat and start to set up my space. Cane and Jack choose seats as far away from me as they can get.

It takes less than fifteen minutes for the pilot to get us cleared and off the ground. The lone flight attendant lets me know when I can turn on my laptop. All three of us finish getting out our various devices and get to work. I'm trying to reach Tiny and see how close he is. Jack is trying to find any team we may have worked with that might be even vaguely close. Cane is coordinating with Kenny on anything we may need as far as tech support goes. It will take us 10 hours to get to the island and I know Tiny will be able to get there in half the time. Either way by the time anyone makes land fall whatever is going on may well be over. This without a doubt is the hardest part and my greatest fear.

I finally reach Tiny; he tells me that they are making good time and he has called everyone and anyone he knows that may be able to get there faster. I know that he has plenty of family on some of the outlying islands. He tells me that as soon as he knows something he will contact me. I'm getting constant notes from the pilot via the flight attendant. She clearly knows something is wrong. She has been with us long enough to wait until she's needed and not to ask too many questions.

At about the four and half hour mark the computer rings. I know it's Tiny. I also know I don't want to hear what he has to tell me.

"Tiny?" is really all I can say when I see his face

appear on my screen. Neither Jack nor Cane get out of their seat.

"We here," he looks down and sighs, "it's a mess. We'll secure the island. Anyone moving will be kept alive and you can make any decisions when you get here. I found him and I will stay with him until you get here"

I take a deep breath. "Thank you".

Tiny nods and disconnects.

I pick up the empty green glass water bottle in front of me and hurl it across the cabin. It smashes into pieces and the only person that moves is the flight attendant. This is not the first time she has had to clean up after me. I stab the light button over my seat, plunging my space into darkness and pull my blanket up over my head. Sleep is the only thing I can manage at the moment. I can hear Cane and Jack loading weapons and this in some strange way gives me great comfort.

The captain's announcement that we are 15 minutes away serves as my wakeup call. I stretch as best I can and make my way to the bathroom. I brush my teeth with the bottled water and put some drops in my eyes. I straighten myself up and head back into the main cabin. When I get back to my seat I find my leg holster, my HK and 2 additional clips laying in it. Also laying in the seat is my Ka-Bar skeleton. Jack and Cane take turns in the bathroom. The landing gear goes down just as we take our seats.

We touch down and Jack is up on his feet and waiting for the plane to stop. When the knock comes from the other side he opens the door. I'm already standing behind him and Cane is quiet behind me. We're down the steps and into the waiting pickups in a matter of minutes. The convoy speeds across the island and they come to a screeching halt at the dock. We're out of the trucks and into the speed boats in record time.

I recognize one of Tiny's many cousins is at the wheel. He nods in hello and we brace ourselves as he pushes down the throttle. I know we reached the island in record time even though it felt like it took hours. The driver slows and I'm about to yell at him when I see what has caused his sudden caution. There are bodies in the water. They're our men and they've been secured to buoys in the water. Floating around them in the water is a lot of debris; in all likelihood the boats they were in.

When we reach the beach, I don't wait for the boat to be pulled further onto the sand. The water is at my calves and it brings on a harsh wave of cold reality. I get to the beach and one of the men points to the main house and puts up two fingers. This tells me that Tiny is on the second floor. I turn and look at Jack he simply nods. I see him grab Cane's arm and say something to him. They both start to talk to Tiny's men as I head into the house. Before the door closes I can hear Jack giving instructions about gathering evidence and collecting the dead.

I can see from the bodies heading up the stairs that our guys gave just as good as they got. I know from their sacrifice we will be able to find out who did this. I call out to Tiny as I reach the top of the stairs. It gives me a moment to collect myself.

"I hear you girlie," comes his <u>k</u>ind baritone voice through the door.

I take a deep breath despite the smell and walk into the room. I see him lying there, on the floor. He put up a fight, I never doubted it. I can only manage to keep him in focus despite the rest of the room. I turn and look up at Tiny with a question on my face.

"I threw the fucker that killed him out the window. I did not want that asshole's spirit mingling with his and I wanted you to be able to be alone with him when you got here."

I know my eyes are filling with tears, so I nod in appreciation. Before the first tear can fall Tiny has left the room and closed the door behind him. Leaving us alone in the room.

About the Author

L.M. Causey resides in Las Vegas and is a graduate of UNLV with a B.A. In Criminal Justice. Being raised in a multi-generational military family, along with travel both local, across the U.S. and abroad have inspired her stories.

New Zealand Rugby, she is a fan of the All Blacks, and was in London in 2015 to watch her favorite team win the World Cup, and WWE are some of her favorite entertainments. Her significant other has introduced her to other favorites: *Family Guy* and *American Dad*.

Music is a big part of her writing process, popular bands being the *Kenny Wayne Shepherd Band* and *Halestorm*.

And yes, she does own an HK .45.

Contact the author at:

Instagram: lisalasvegas777

Twitter: @LisaLasVegas777

Facebook: L.M. Causey